PATTERNS IN THE SNOW

Peter Clark had taken Nicci's heart and broken it in the cruellest way imaginable. So when Nicci and her best friend Karen treated themselves to a skiing holiday in Switzerland it should have been a happy interlude. However, it soon turned into a catalogue of disasters for Nicci. Time and again she crossed swords with sour-tempered Andrew Thornton, never once dreaming that he would eventually turn out to be the best medicine she could hope to have.

JANET WHITEHEAD

PATTERNS IN THE SNOW

Complete and Unabridged

LINFORD
Leicester

First published in Great Britain in 1991

First Linford Edition
published 2007

British Library CIP Data

Whitehead, Janet
  Patterns in the snow.—Large print ed.—
Linford romance library
  1. Love stories
  2. Large type books
  I. Title
  823.9'14 [F]

ISBN 978–1–84782–037–2

Published by
F. A. Thorpe (Publishing)
Anstey, Leicestershire

Set by Words & Graphics Ltd.
Anstey, Leicestershire
Printed and bound in Great Britain by
T. J. International Ltd., Padstow, Cornwall

This book is printed on acid-free paper

Dedicated to Ruby McConnell,
in sincere appreciation of all her
interest and encouragement

1

'All right, Nicci, you can relax now,' Karen Payne said good-naturedly. 'We've landed at last.'

Nicci Salter glanced sideways at her travelling companion and smiled ruefully. 'Was it that obvious that I'd never flown before?' she asked, leaning forward to get her first glimpse of Zurich through the small square window to her left.

Karen was already unbuckling her safety belt, anxious to move around a little after the ninety-minute flight from Heathrow. 'Only to my trained eye,' she replied.

Well, Nicci certainly couldn't deny her relief that the bulk of their trip was over. At first, when Karen had suggested they take a skiing holiday in Switzerland, it had seemed like a good idea. After that awful, soul-destroying

1

business with Peter Clark, Nicci's spirits had been at a seriously low ebb. Her confidence had deserted her, and she had known she must do something to regain that precious sense of self-worth. But as the time for their holiday grew nearer, Nicci had started to have doubts.

Oh, she knew that Karen had suggested the break with the best of intentions, and she loved her friend dearly for it. But shouldn't she just face up to the situation instead of run away from it? After all, this holiday would change nothing. When their two weeks here in Switzerland came to an end, she would be back where she started, in the same, all-too-familiar environment, trying to live down the embarrassment Peter had caused her.

She knew it was wrong to start the holiday with misgivings. She must try to enjoy it, for Karen's sake. But she had a nasty feeling that it wasn't going to be easy.

'Come on, lazy bones,' Karen said,

giving her a nudge that shook her from her reverie. 'Time's a-wastin' — and our holiday starts right *here*.'

Nicci summoned a brief, uncertain smile and unbuckled her own safety belt. 'All right, Captain, lead on. You're the one with the guidebook.'

Shortly after the plane taxied to a halt on one of Kloten Airport's many runways, the passengers began to debark in a long, orderly line. The day was bright and clear, the February sunshine weak but nonetheless welcome.

A bus took them all swiftly across the tarmac to one of the terminals, where they joined an apparently endless flow of people trying to reclaim their luggage, and Nicci and Karen waited patiently for their own knapsacks and light cases to appear on the slow-moving conveyor belt.

The two girls were of a similar age. Karen was twenty-four, Nicci eighteen months older. They had also dressed in a similar fashion for the journey, casually in padded jackets over open-necked blouses and jeans. Nicci was five feet eight, and her body was slim and graceful. She wore her naturally wavy auburn hair nape-length, and her bright hazel eyes reflected both intelligence and a kind nature. She had a small, snubbed nose and a full, heart-shaped mouth, and when she smiled her whole face lit up. She hadn't smiled much since the beginning of October, however. Not since Peter —

'At last!' said Karen.

'Eh?'

'My knapsack. Here it comes now. See it?'

'How could I miss it?' Nicci replied teasingly. 'The blessed thing's fluorescent pink!'

Karen was Nicci's complete opposite. She was slightly shorter than her friend, and often embarrassing in her direct-ness. She had a luxuriant shock of natural blonde hair and the most perfect blue eyes Nicci had ever seen.

In temperament the girls differed,

4

too. Karen was brash, outward-going and something of a comedienne. Sometimes Nicci felt that Karen's whole life was devoted only to having a good time. She, by contrast, was quieter than her friend, more sensitive and given to introspection.

Perhaps that was the secret of their friendship, though. Maybe deep down, each of them admired the traits of the other. Certainly, they'd hit it off from the very first day that Karen had come to work with her in the accounts department of a small North London firm that manufactured electrical components.

Gathering up their baggage, the girls moved on through Customs (a mere formality, since they had nothing to declare). Outside, finding a relatively quiet spot to one side of all the chaos, they paused to look at the city through the heavy glass façade of the airport.

Nicci had been uncertain as to what to expect from Zurich, but what she saw now more than matched up to her expectations. Charming old buildings stood side by side with gleaming new ones. Just across the busy street she saw a park resplendent with a whole profusion of flowers that fairly took her breath away. Dominating everything, however, were the majestic, snow-capped peaks soaring skyward in the far, misty distance.

'It's beautiful,' Nicci breathed, almost to herself.

'Yes, he is,' Karen agreed.

Nicci frowned. ''He'?'

She glanced quizzically at her friend, to find her smiling at someone off to their left. When she followed Karen's gaze, she saw two handsome young Zurchers, as the inhabitants of the city were known, grinning back at them from the other side of the terminal. One of them waved, and Karen waved back.

Watching the display, Nicci gave a theatrical sigh. 'Karen, you're incorrigible! We've only been here half an hour and already you've started working your way through the entire male population of Switzerland!'

'Only those under the age of thirty,' Karen replied, still distracted.

Much to Nicci's alarm, she indicated that the Zurchers should come over and join them, but one of them assumed a disappointed look and pointed first to his wristwatch, then in the general direction of the runways.

'Oh, too bad,' Karen said. 'Looks as if they're leaving just as we've arrived.'

The young blonde girl finally tore her attention away from the two men when they disappeared into the crowd. 'Now,' she said, turning to look up at Nicci. 'What was that you were saying about me being insatiable?'

'In*corrigible*,' Nicci corrected. 'Though I wonder if your word mightn't be more apt.'

Karen only chuckled. 'I'm starving,' she said. 'What say we go and get something to eat at that restaurant over there?'

Nicci nodded. 'Come on, then.'

As near as they could estimate by making a few hurried mental calculations, the restaurant, or, to be more accurate, the cafeteria, appeared to be quite inexpensive. They went inside, checked the predominantly German-sounding menu and helped themselves to trays. Although she too was feeling a little hungry after the flight, Nicci was content to have a sandwich and some coffee. Karen, being Karen, decided she must try the cafeteria's speciality, something long and complicated that started with a Z and sounded just like a sneeze when she tried to pronounce it.

It took them a few confused moments to work out exactly how many Swiss francs the woman at the cash register was asking for, but once that was behind them they found a small, spotless table close to a window where they could continue to gaze out at the bustling streets.

'Are you all right with that?' Nicci asked as she unwrapped her sandwich.

Karen looked up from the meal she had just purchased. She had been looking at the mixture of veal, beef, liver, sweetbreads and vegetables as if she were seriously doubting the wisdom of her choice. But then, bravely, she picked up her fork and set to. 'Sure,' she replied confidently.

'Where's the guidebook?' Nicci asked, taking a sip of coffee.

Karen finished chewing. 'What's your hurry?'

'No hurry. I just think I'll feel a bit more settled when we reach Anderberg, that's all.'

Karen's perfect blue eyes twinkled. 'Can't wait to get the old skis on, eh?'

Nicci grimaced. 'I'm dreading that, as well you know.'

'But there's nothing to it,' Karen insisted. Unlike Nicci, she had skied before, both at home and abroad, and loved it. 'It's easy. Really. Just like falling off a log.'

Nicci eyed her over the edge of her sandwich. 'I wish you'd chosen a different expression,' she said, deadpan. 'Now — the guidebook?'

With her free hand, Karen took a dog-eared paperback from one of the

pockets of her fluorescent pink knapsack and passed it over. 'There's no
need to concern yourself,' she said in
between forkfuls of meat and vegetable.
'I've got it all worked out. First of all,
we've got to get to the mainline railway
station, the Humpty — something-or-
other — '

'The *Hauptbahnhof*,' said Nicci.

'That's the one,' Karen agreed,
spearing a slice of carrot. 'There should
be an underground train that'll take us
there somewhere around here.'

'There is,' Nicci cut in, glancing up
from the guidebook. 'Right beneath
where we're sitting.'

'Oh, right.' Karen swallowed and reached
for her own cup of coffee. 'Well, when
we get to the Humpty-whatever-you-
called-it, we have to get a mainline train
to Saint-something-or-other. That goes
right through Anderberg.'

'The Saint Gotthard route,' Nicci
said, closing the book.

Karen smiled at her and resumed
eating. 'There, you see?' she said. 'I told

you I had it all worked out, didn't I?'

After they finished eating, the two friends gathered up their luggage and set out to find the subway. By now, however, the terminal had grown increasingly busy, and as they stood there, searching for the right direction to take, they found all the signs positively bewildering.

'Oh, this is getting us nowhere,' Karen announced after a moment. 'I'll ask someone for directions.' Producing the dog-eared guidebook again, she hastily flipped through to the handy German phrases listed at the back. 'Ah, this one ought to do the trick,' she decided a moment later.

Together the friends peered around in search of someone to ask. A tall man with a rugged, sober face and wind-swept, very dark brown hair was coming their way, his hands stuffed into the pockets of his grey overcoat and a scarf tied around his neck against the chill of the day. To Nicci he did not look like a particularly happy man. In fact, if his scowl was anything to go by, he seemed rather short-tempered.

Of all the people from whom she could have sought directions, however, it was just like Karen to pick him.

When he was near enough, she stepped straight into his path, making him come to a sudden, surprised halt.

'Er . . . *verzeihung*,' she said, reading from the guidebook.

The man looked down at her, stern-faced and obviously in a hurry. '*Ja?*'

Karen formed the words slowly, and with great effort. '*Wo . . . ist . . . der . . . Bahnhof, bitte?*'

To their surprise, a faint, disparaging smile touched the man's lips. 'With an accent as dreadful as that,' he said in a deep and cultured voice, 'you've just got to be from England.'

Even Karen was taken aback by his bluntness, for it was obvious that he did not mean his observation to be taken as a joke, and Nicci, standing nearby, found herself bristling uncharacteristically at the sarcasm in his tone.

'Ah . . . why, yes, we are,' Karen muttered. 'I, ah . . . I was asking — '

'I know what you were asking for,' the man interrupted, his tanned, weathered face still unsmiling. 'And the subway is right over there — by the sign that says 'Subway'.'

He could not have made them feel more foolish had he tried. Before either of the girls could comment on his rudeness, however, he said, 'Now, if you'll excuse me . . . ' And so saying, he brushed past them to continue on his way.

'Charmed, I'm sure,' Karen muttered to his retreating back. 'Well, if that's an example of Swiss manners — '

Nicci, still watching him stride purposefully off through the crowd, said, 'But he wasn't Swiss. Didn't you hear his accent? He was English.'

Karen shrugged. 'Swiss, English, what's the difference? Bad manners are bad manners wherever you find them.'

There was no arguing with that, so without another word the girls scooped up their luggage once again and set off across the gleaming terminal.

A short while later they reached the ticket office and Nicci asked for two one-way tickets to the *Hauptbahnhof*. Again there was some confusion over the amount they were required to pay, for they were unused to the strange coins and notes they'd obtained before leaving home, and uncertain about the various denominations of all their francs and *rappen*.

The confusion grew even worse when Nicci accidentally dropped her purse and spilled coins all over the tiled floor.

'Oh dear . . . '

Bending, she hurriedly scooped them back up, examining the selection in her open palm. 'Now, let me see . . . '

'Oh, for heaven's sake, can't you get a move on!'

Finding the irritable voice behind them familiar, both Nicci and Karen glanced around. Directly behind Karen stood the rugged-faced man who had just directed them to the subway.

Judging from the newspaper he carried under one arm, he had stopped off at one of the airport's many news-stands before coming down to purchase a ticket of his own.

'I'm sorry,' Nicci said stiffly. 'I'll be as quick as I can.'

'You're holding everyone up,' the man said, although he was the only one waiting. 'What's the matter, anyway?'

'Nothing that need concern you,' said Karen, defensively.

'Oh, but it *does* concern me,' the man snapped angrily. 'All your messing about's going to make me late!'

'What for?' Karen enquired acidly. 'Your appointment at the charm school?'

The man's lips thinned down danger-ously and he drew in a deep breath. Somehow he bit off a sarcastic rejoin-der.

Stepping around Karen, he reached down and took hold of Nicci's hand. His touch was surprisingly gentle, and the skin of his fingertips was warm and smooth. For a moment Nicci felt a tingle wash over her, but that was probably because his actions had taken her by surprise.

'Right,' he snapped in a very business-like way. 'How much do you need?'

Nicci glanced up into his weathered face. He was perhaps thirty years old, certainly no more, though his depthless grey eyes appeared tired, somehow troubled, the eyes of a much older man.

'Well?' he prodded.

She named the figure, and using his other hand, the man quickly selected the correct amount from the coins in her palm.

'There,' he said, passing them to the waiting ticket clerk. 'Now perhaps the rest of us can get a look in at last.'

Nicci felt heat rushing to her face. She licked her lips. She wanted to give this arrogant man a piece of her mind. Still, he was right to be angry, she supposed. She and Karen *had* held him up, albeit unintentionally. Besides . . . it was peculiar, she knew, but somehow she sensed that he was not really angry at her, but at something else, something against which he was powerless.

For one timeless moment she stared up at him. Dimly she realised that he still had hold of her hand. She opened her mouth to say something, but then the contact between them was broken and the man was turning his attention to the ticket clerk and requesting his own ticket.

Nicci felt Karen's hand on her arm, leading her away from him. 'It's all right, love,' she said in a low, venomous tone. 'Don't upset yourself. He ought to pick on someone his own size, the big bully.'

Nicci blinked. 'Upset?' she repeated. 'I'm not upset.'

'You're kidding. You've gone as white as a sheet.'

The girls began to head towards the platform just as a train thundered in. 'I'm not upset, though,' Nicci insisted. 'Just curious.'

'What, about Attila the Hun back

there?' Karen snorted. 'I don't want to worry you, Nic, but I think you must be suffering from jet lag.'

★ ★ ★

The mainline station proved to be no more than a ten-minute ride away. After some searching, they located the train they had to catch to Anderberg and hurried aboard just a minute or so before it began to slide gracefully from the station.

Although it picked up speed once the *Hauptbahnhof* lay behind them, the train continued to trundle southward at a slow clip. The girls didn't mind this in the least, though, because it gave them a chance to see some sights as they crossed the Zurichsee, or Lake of Zurich, and began to wind steadily up and over the wrinkled land.

After a while Nicci began to relax. Although she had doubted that a fortnight in this admittedly beautiful country would mend the heart Peter

Clark had broken so cruelly, she now felt that the change of scene would certainly help to speed up the healing process.

For a moment she pictured Peter in her mind. His name and image were never far from her thoughts, anyway. She saw him brushing his fine blond hair back off his forehead, caught the ivory flash of his winning smile and the dangerously attractive sparkle in his clear blue eyes, and she remembered them all so clearly that it was difficult to imagine that nearly three months had elapsed since she'd last seen him.

Peter was tall and athletic, witty, urbane and personable. She had loved him with a passion she had never dreamed she could possess. But *was* it love, or mere infatuation? As events grew vague and blurred with the passage of time, she could no longer be sure.

'Mint?' Karen asked, offering a packet of sweets she'd picked up back at Heathrow.

19

Nicci shook her head, sending a shiver through her wavy auburn hair. 'No thanks.' Then she returned her gaze to the wide window beside her, and stared out past her thoughtful reflection at the passing countryside.

According to their map, Anderberg lay some fifty miles to the south. At the speed they were travelling, it looked as if they were in for a long but comfortable ride. The land was breath-taking, and filled with colour; from green meadows filled with wild flowers to the distant, snow-covered summits of, among others, the Eiger. Even the lakes they passed were picturesque, their surfaces, reflecting the clear blue sky above, ruffled occasionally by a sharp winter breeze.

Before long Karen closed her eyes and tried to sleep. Admiration of so much wild beauty was not for her. She wanted only to reach Anderberg, settle her luggage in their room, then check out the ski slopes — and the men.

Nicci smiled fondly over at her

dozing companion. Karen was like elastic, she thought. No matter how far she stretched her emotions, they always snapped right back into place. If only it had been the same for her . . .

At last the guard appeared in the corridor beyond their compartment, checking tickets as he went and calling out the names of the stations as they approached them. Little over an hour later the girls heard his voice announcing their destination, and with a flutter of excitement in their stomachs they gathered up their luggage and peered expectantly through the window.

Anderberg came into view around a wide, lazy bend in the tracks.

The little resort was nestled amid towering slopes that rose tall and craggy to the north and south. Nicci thought it looked just like a Christmas card illustration. The streets were narrow and cobbled, most of the chalets of typical Swiss design, with low, sloping roofs and small windows. The pavements were merely thin grey ribbons of stone, along which strolled tourists and townsfolk alike. The roads, however, were relatively quiet. Traffic was light, and confined to the odd car or bright yellow bus.

'*Look*!' Karen squealed like a child. Nicci followed her pointing finger. 'Our hotel!'

Their destination, the Hotel Anderberg, was a large, pine-panelled building overlooking the town from a green, thickly-forested slope on the far side of the valley. Despite its size, and the fact that it stood four storeys high, its rustic, typically Alpine appearance at once made them feel welcome.

Just to the left of the hotel they spotted tiny, heavily-clothed figures descending an artificial ski slope in a series of graceful curves. To one side of the slope, a number of basic T-bar lifts were taking yet more skiers back to the top for another heady descent.

'Isn't it marvellous?' Karen breathed excitedly.

Nicci had to agree. It was wonderful,

a fairy-tale land that was a lifetime away from the home in Eastcote she shared with her widowed mother and younger sister, or the office they both worked in back in London.

The train slowly pulled into Anderberg Station, and the girls climbed out into a crisp but sunny Swiss afternoon. Standing just inside the station entrance, Karen asked Nicci how she thought they should get to the hotel. Before she could reply, however, the rugged-faced man with whom they'd had such trouble back in Zurich suddenly brushed past them and walked off up the street, hands firmly shoved into the pockets of his grey overcoat, shoulders hunched against the breeze, head downcast, as if in deep and serious thought.

'Nic?' Karen prompted. 'Hello? Anybody there?'

With effort Nicci tore her curious gaze from the man's retreating back. 'I'm sorry?'

'How should we get up to the hotel?' Karen asked again. 'By taxi, one of those buses that looks more like a banana on wheels, or Shanks's pony?'

Nicci shrugged. 'I don't know. Whichever's easiest,' she replied, still distracted.

'Taxi, then,' Karen decided with unholy relish. 'Let's turn up at the Anderberg in style.'

2

Although they had, by necessity, chosen a modest hotel, the Anderberg proved to be even more grand inside than it was from without. In addition to the elegant combination bar and lounge the girls noticed as they crossed the reception, the hotel also boasted a swimming-pool, sauna and solarium.

The room to which they were shown, however, was fairly small, although they agreed that it was good enough for their purposes. After all, if Karen had anything to do with it, they would be out on the slopes for most of the days, and sampling the resort's night-life after dark.

At the moment, though, the girls just wanted to unwind. At last the rigours of the day were making themselves felt, and taking off their jackets, Nicci went over to the window to sample the view while Karen stretched out on one of the two single beds.

Suddenly Karen chuckled. 'That taxi worked out to be a bit expensive, didn't it? I think we'd have been better off catching the bus.'

Nicci nodded her agreement. The window gave her a commanding view of the hotel grounds, the artificial ski slope and the mountain slopes beyond, which for some reason, the skiers were avoiding.

In the opposite direction lay the town. From this distance and elevation, it looked just like the type of village you might find on a model railway. Just on its southernmost fringe rose a square building with a flat roof, which had been constructed at the foot of yet more shelving, ragged-edged mountains. The building stood three storeys high, with red-brick walls and powder-blue paintwork. Nicci wondered what it was.

'Gosh, my back's killing me,' Karen complained. 'It's carrying that knapsack that did it.' When Nicci still made no verbal reply, she paused, studying her friend's silhouette against the gradually paling sky. 'Nic? Are you all right? You've gone all quiet.'

Nicci turned away from the window to face her, a vaguely embarrassed smile on her full lips. 'I'm fine. Just . . . just thinking.'

Karen propped herself up on one elbow, her frown a frown of concern. 'Not about Peter — the rat?'

'Oh, no,' Nicci said quickly.

Karen saw right through her denial, though. She had seen the symptoms before. 'Come on, love. You can't fool me. Get it off your chest, if it'll make you feel any easier.'

Nicci sat on the edge of the other bed and shrugged. 'No, let's change the subject. We're on holiday, after all. We should be enjoying ourselves.'

Karen sat up and looked her straight in the face. 'Right. First things first, then. Let's get showered and changed, and see what we can do about hiring some skiing equipment for tomorrow.'

Nicci nodded, determined to make the best of things. 'All right. Maybe we can make some enquiries at the ski shop about enrolling me in a beginner's course, too.'

Karen gave her a withering glance. 'What do you need with a course? *I'll* teach you all you need to know.'

Nicci eyed her dubiously. 'Are you sure?'

'Sure I'm sure. Trust me. We'll call it 'Karen's Course'.'

Finally Nicci smiled. 'All right,' she said. 'Just so long as 'Karen's Course' doesn't turn out to be a 'crash' course!'

★　★　★

By the time they'd finished hiring all their ski-wear and equipment, the girls were famished. Darkness had come early to the valley, and all over the town windows glowed with a cheery amber welcome. After dinner at the hotel restaurant, they decided to go for a walk and explore the narrow streets.

Anderberg was surprisingly active after dark. Nicci had half-expected the resort to be a sleepy little backwater, but nothing could have been further from the truth. There was quite an array of shops, all of which opened late, three or four cafés and restaurants and at least twice as many bars and discos. There was also an ice rink, a gymnasium and a whole assortment of souvenir shops.

The evening had brought a distinct drop in temperature with it, and the girls were glad that their jackets zipped right up to the throat.

On impulse, Karen dragged Nicci into a *stubli* bar and ordered two glasses of home-made punch, even though she knew that Nicci drank only rarely. 'To celebrate the start of an unforgettable holiday,' she said, grinning.

They found a corner table and sat down. An open fire crackled pleasantly on the other side of the crowded, pine-panelled room, and music issued from a juke-box near the door. The *stubli* bar appeared to be frequented mainly by holiday-makers, which was only to be expected, of course, and the buzz of chatter was warm and welcoming.

The girls clinked their glasses and Nicci said, 'To the holiday of a lifetime.'

It was to be quite a prophetic toast.

'It's nice here, isn't it?' Karen remarked, taking a sip of the strong, citrus-scented punch. 'In Anderberg, I mean.'

'It's lovely,' Nicci agreed. 'But . . . '

'What?'

'Well, I could be wrong, of course, but . . . ' Nicci gave a shrug. 'Considering that this is supposed to be a ski resort — where's all the snow?'

Karen gave her a blank look. 'Snow?'

'Yes. The streets and roofs are all bone-dry, and the mountains themselves look quite bare except for one or two odd patches.'

Karen obviously hadn't noticed the

town's peculiar absence of snow until this moment. She gave Nicci's observation a moment or two's thought, then took another sip from her glass. 'Maybe it's late this year,' she finally decided. 'You know how unpredictable the weather's become just lately.'

'If you ask me, it's not coming at all this year.'

The two girls turned to find a young, dark-skinned man in his early twenties regarding them through dark, smiling eyes. He had been sitting at the next table with some friends when he had obviously overheard their conversation. Now he spoke quite knowledgeably. 'These places can generally rely on a good three feet of snow right at the start of the season,' he said. 'But this year — or rather, the end of *last* year — something somewhere went a bit wrong. There's been no snow in Anderberg now for, oh, at least eight months.'

'None at all?' Karen asked despondently.

'Not a flake, I'm afraid,' said the young man. Suddenly he smiled at them and extended his right hand. 'My name's Leno, by the way. Leno de Masi. I supervise a few advanced skiing classes up at the Anderberg Hotel.'

The girls introduced themselves as they shook his hand.

Leno was dressed in a thick sweater and padded grey trousers. He had a square, reliable face with a shadow of stubble along his firm jaw, and he wore his medium-length, raven-black hair in a kind of untamed, finger-combed style that suited him well. Although he was seated, he looked as if he might be tall. He was certainly athletic, and blessed with the good looks so typical among young Mediterranean men.

'I imagine this dry weather must be bad for business,' said Nicci.

'It is,' Leno replied. 'Oh, there's always the artificial slopes, of course, and we've started running coaches out to the Oberalp Pass, where they've been disgustingly lucky for snow, but it's a shame, really. Around here we have some of the finest runs in central Switzerland, and not just for down-slope skiing, either. We have cross-country trails that stretch for more than thirty kilometres above the tree-line.'

Karen was impressed — and clearly smitten. 'I must say, ah, Leno. Your English is perfect.'

Leno shrugged and gave an assured smile. 'It should be. I've spent practically my whole life growing up around English tourists, first in the resorts we have back home in Italy, then here.' He eyed the girls speculatively. 'Do *you* ski, or is this your first time?'

Before Nicci could open her mouth, Karen cut in. 'Actually, I'm a fairly advanced student myself,' she said, trying to impress the Italian.

Leno raised one eyebrow. 'Maybe I'll see you out on the dry slope tomorrow, then? I'm up there practically every day.'

As the two of them continued their conversation, Nicci took another sip of punch. She was glad that her friend had found a man she liked, but that only made her feel more uncomfortable. That she was unintentionally playing gooseberry couldn't be helped, though. It would look odd — and just a bit obvious — if she excused herself now. The only thing she could do was gradually fade into the background and allow Karen to take centre-stage.

She turned her attention to the *stubli* bar's other patrons as Karen and Leno continued to swap ski stories. Although she would never admit it, Nicci didn't think it very likely that she would ever share her friend's passion for the sport, and in any case, much of what they were saying about 'counter rotation' and 'inside skiing' might just as well have been a foreign language.

It was as she was sitting quietly to one side that she noticed a tall man standing up at the bar. Although he had his back to her, he was so similar to Peter in both build and colouring that she felt her heart leap and beat faster.

At once she hated herself for still allowing him to dominate her thoughts, and wishing that she could relive those good times they'd shared together.

But earlier on Karen had called Peter a rat, and thinking about it now, Nicci realised that her description hadn't really been too far off the mark. Because Peter had taken her love and trust and abused them both, cruelly and with no thought for the consequences.

Nicci had first met Peter at work. Peter had been one of the company's two sales reps, and he was always popping into the accounts department to check whether certain invoices had been sent out or paid, and to confirm special arrangements or discounts he had agreed with their customers.

His charm and personality had made him an ideal choice for his job. He had a way with words and could doubtless have sold sand to the Arabs had he put his mind to it. Inevitably, the more Nicci saw of him, the more she found about him to like.

After a while they'd started dating. Peter was attentive and thoughtful, and seemed genuinely interested in all her hopes and ambitions for the future. Nicci had had boyfriends in the past, of course, but Peter's maturity, coupled with an obviously caring attitude, set him apart from all the rest.

She realised now that she had chosen to ignore his faults, which were many. Sometimes he would drop out of sight for an afternoon, or fail to call her for several days at a time, but he always had a plausible excuse — and that confident, winning smile, of course — with which to smooth things over.

But then he started asking about the petty cash box in Nicci's desk drawer, and taking the odd five or ten-pound note as an advance against expenses, never stopping long enough to sign an IOU.

Once he told her that he was visiting some electrical wholesalers in Derbyshire for a week. When he sent his time- and mileage-sheets in a month later, she saw that he had in fact taken a week's leave. When she mentioned that to him, he grew angry and accused her of spying on him. When she asked him to repay the money he had taken from the petty cash box before the company auditors came in to check the books, he said that she didn't trust him, and promptly dropped out of sight again.

In the end, Nicci repaid the money — forty pounds — from her own savings.

Now, taking another sip of the strong punch, she realised what a fool she'd been. She had loved Peter with an intensity that had surprised and delighted her. For all his failings, he was so attractive, and his soft, gentle words of love always made her feel secure and wanted . . . But now she knew that he had used her, again and again, and just like a fool she had always gone back for more.

As the weeks turned into months, their relationship had grown more and more strained. Again Peter asked for an advance from the petty cash box, and against her better judgement she had given in to him. Six weeks later she was forced once again to repay the loan — this time totalling sixty pounds — from her own funds.

Then one day a secretary from the sales department came in with a card for her to sign. 'Who's leaving?' she had asked, studying the design on the front.

The answer had come as a chilling double-blow that even now left her numb and faintly nauseous. 'Peter. Didn't you know? He's going to work for his fiancée's father, selling double glazing or something.'

Knowing Nicci's feelings for Peter, the girls on the other side of the office had fallen silent. Karen, too, had felt something go cold in the pit of her stomach.

After a moment Nicci had found her voice and said weakly, 'F . . . fiancée?'

The secretary had nodded, still blissfully unaware of the bombshell she'd just dropped. 'Gosh, you don't get to hear much tucked away up here, do you? They've been engaged for almost a year now, getting married in a couple of months. That's why her dad's taken him into the family business at last, if you ask me . . . '

Suddenly the girl noticed how pale Nicci had grown, and how quiet and concerned the normally-exuberant Karen had become, and she began to sense that something was very badly wrong. 'I'll, ah, I'll come back later, if you like,' she said awkwardly.

But she never did come back.

For a long while after that Nicci just stared down at her typewriter. Well, she supposed in that odd, distant way that people always react to bad news, at least that explained Peter's periodic absences. He'd been spending time with the woman he was going to marry! Feeling crushed and dejected, Nicci realised for the first time exactly what she had meant to him — a way of obtaining the odd few pounds, that was all, just someone to pander to his ego . . .

By the end of that day, practically the whole company knew the story of how Peter — charming, thoughtful Peter — had used her. Nicci never did find out which of her workmates had spread the gossip, but one of them had, and then her humiliation had become complete.

It had been a hard, hard time, she remembered. Had it not been for the love of her mother and sister, and the support and kindness of Karen, Nicci doubted that she would have come through it.

Not that it was entirely behind her even now, she reminded herself, watching the motion of her trembling hand as she put the punch-glass back on the table.

★ ★ ★

Early the following morning the girls donned their ski-suits and collected their skis from the shop adjoining the hotel. Once again the day was crisp and clear, the sky blue and cloudless and the sunshine weak but welcome. At first Nicci felt awkward on her skis. They were much longer than she had expected, although Karen assured her that she would soon get used to them.

Together they headed for the T-bar lifts taking their fellow skiers up the artificial, or dry, slope. Already there were holiday-makers everywhere, some surprisingly proficient, others even more awkward on their skis than Nicci.

'We'll start you off on the basics, I think,' Karen decided, studying Nicci's somewhat apprehensive profile through colourful goggles. 'So don't worry, we won't be trying anything too adventurous today.'

'Not even if it means attracting Leno's attention?' Nicci teased, smiling at her as the T-bar began to lift them smoothly up the mountain.

'Leno?' Karen repeated, feigning puzzlement. 'Who's Leno?'

'Do you mean to say you've forgotten?' Nicci asked sceptically. 'You were drooling over him enough last night.'

'Oh, *that* Leno,' Karen said with a laugh. 'Well, I don't suppose there's much chance of bumping into him at the lower elevations, but if we *should* see him . . . '

'I know, I know. I promise to make myself scarce.'

'There's a good girl.'

Much to Nicci's surprise, Karen proved to be a patient, if sarcastic, teacher, and together they spent an exhausting morning on the lower slopes, as far away from the other skiers as possible, just going over the preliminaries.

At first it was a minor triumph just getting Nicci to stand upright on the slope for any length of time. Her sense of balance seemed to desert her over and over again, although once she finally found her 'ski legs', she grew considerably more confident.

Rather like a driving instructor, Karen went through every procedure in a clear and concise way. Occasionally she would demonstrate a particular technique, and Nicci saw that she was indeed a reasonably advanced student of the sport.

In fact, her skill made Nicci feel exactly like the awkward novice she was, but she stuck at it, although the muscles in her legs and lower back ached terribly, and set about trying to master the art of starting, stopping and turning.

At last, some time towards the middle of the day, she made her first proper descent of the artificial slope. Admittedly, they were only some thirty feet from level ground, and Nicci's speed was slow and given to all sorts of kangaroo hops, but once she felt the cool, slightly damp wind against her face and in her hair, she felt an exhilaration she hadn't known for months.

'That looked pretty reasonable to me,' Karen announced a short while later, skiing down to join her. 'How did it feel?'

Nicci considered before replying. 'A

43

bit wobbly at first, until I got the hang of it.'

'Well, don't forget to use your legs. The skis won't take you where you want to go unless you use your legs and feet to control them.'

Nicci nodded. 'I understand.'

'That's what I like to hear — confidence! Come on, race you to the T-bars!'

'What, like this?'

'All right, then. We'll plod.'

They trudged back to the lifts and ascended the slope again. This time, however, Karen took them just a shade higher than before, and much to her surprise, Nicci found that she didn't mind this in the least.

The slopes held a happy, carefree atmosphere. For almost as far as she could see, brightly-clad tourists in large and small groups were having the time of their lives. Everywhere she looked she saw smiling faces, and men, women and children talking animatedly. A few poor souls kept falling over in a wild tangle of arms, legs and skis, but they always got back up, dusted themselves off and set out all over again. In all, it was a wonderful panorama, and it filled Nicci with a sense of tranquillity and contentment, as if everything really *were* all right in the world.

Such was her new-found enthusiasm that she and Karen continued her tuition right through lunch-time, stopping only once to buy a glass of orange squash at one of the slope shops. After that it was back to the T-bars, and another slow ascent of the incline.

This time Karen took her still higher up the slope, where the more proficient skiers whispered gracefully past with knees bent, heads up and poles tucked firmly under their arms. Before they could resume their instruction, however, their attention was taken by a man in a one-piece ski-suit wearing goggles and a sweat-band, who flashed by and promptly executed a number of complex moves for their benefit. He twisted this way and that, seemingly without effort, and finally came around in a wide arc that brought him to within ten or twelve feet of the girls.

'*Leno!*' Karen said, offering him an appreciative little hand-clap. 'That was marvellous!'

The Italian ski instructor came to a halt before them with a grin on his face. He was, as they'd suspected the previous night, quite tall, and in the bright sunshine his good looks were even more evident. He nodded a greeting, then said, 'I thought I spotted you two down here. There's no mistaking that blonde hair of yours, Karen.'

Where the compliment would most probably have made Nicci blush furiously, Karen took it completely in her stride. 'We wondered if we'd be seeing you today,' she replied. 'What are you doing down here with the riff-raff, anyway? You should be further up there, shouldn't you, with the *créme de la créme*.'

He chuckled. 'That's the good thing

about running advanced ski classes,' he said. 'Your students are all so good that they hardly need any tuition.'

'Not like me,' Nicci said. 'I'm afraid Karen's had to teach me all morning.'

'From what I saw, it looks as if she's done a good job,' Leno remarked politely. 'Perhaps you'll come up to the higher elevations sometime, and I'll show you a few tricks.'

'Any excuse to show off, eh?' teased Karen.

'But of course,' the handsome Italian replied with a laugh.

'I'll tell you what,' said Nicci, keeping to her earlier promise. 'Why don't you go on up with Leno now, Karen? I think I've had enough of skiing for one day, anyway.'

'Are you sure?'

'Positive. I'll see you back at the hotel later on.'

Karen's smile immediately broadened, and just before she pulled her goggles back down over her eyes she winked and mouthed the words, 'Good girl.'

Nicci watched the pair of them ski off towards the T-bars. She knew that she would have to work hard to become as expert as her friend. Still, she'd made fair progress today, so she couldn't grumble.

Turning her attention back to the slope, she suddenly realised that she was now going to have to make her own descent unsupervised, and felt a faint stirring of unease in her tummy. Just knowing that Karen was on hand had somehow increased her confidence. Now, realising that she was all alone half-way up a slope full of strangers who had no idea how new she was to skiing, made her feel a little cold and apprehensive.

Still, she knew she couldn't just stand here for the rest of the day, or wait until someone took pity on her and offered to nurse her down the gradient. In any case, she doubted sincerely that she would be able to take such an embarrassment. So she quickly ran through as much of what Karen had told her as she could remember, then took a deep, deep breath and used her poles to start her moving very slowly.

Once again, her skis seemed to have a will of their own, and she fought to control them with the muscles in her legs, as Karen had instructed. Although she tried to keep on a roughly straight course, and maintain a safe and steady pace, however, she felt herself speeding up and veering a little to the right.

Now the wind brushing past her face and slipping through her hair felt anything but pleasurable. As her speed increased and her course grew even more erratic, so she found herself having to fight against a rising swell of panic as well.

Her vision, through the goggles, grew jarred and indistinct. The tension in her legs was becoming unbearable. Desperately she tried to recall everything Karen had told her about controlling direction and speed, but Karen had said so much since they'd first come out onto the slopes, and if anything she was now rushing downslope even faster than before . . .

Another skier suddenly appeared in her path, and she opened her mouth to yell a warning to him, but her throat had dried up and all that came out was a croak. It didn't matter, though. The skier, perhaps sensing the imminent collision, glanced over his shoulder at precisely that moment, and Nicci saw the lines in his forehead suddenly deepen as his eyes, behind all-concealing goggles, went wide in disbelief.

Within a matter of seconds they collided, and Nicci felt her breath leave her in a rush. The next few seconds were a confused jumble. She felt the impact mainly in her chest and tumbled over. She believed she did cry out then, and squeezed her eyes tightly shut as she fell to earth with yet another bump that awoke fresh pain.

At last the world stopped spinning and she opened her eyes. She was sprawled on her back, skis slanted sideways like saplings bending to the force of a hurricane. As near as she could estimate, she had suffered no broken bones.

Pushing up her goggles, she glanced around to check on the skier with whom she'd collided, but he was nowhere in sight.

Then the ground beneath her shifted slightly, and she gave a startled yelp.

'*Oh!*'

Rolling to one side, she realised with a sudden hot flush of embarrassment that she hadn't seen the other skier because she'd landed on *top* of him!

Struggling up onto her knees in a most unladylike fashion, she immediately began to offer an apology. 'I'm terribly sorry, I don't know how I can apologise enough . . . Are you all right? Don't move until — '

'I'm all right, woman, just get *off* me!'

As the other skier sat up and pushed his own goggles up onto his forehead, Nicci recognised the rugged-faced man with whom she and Karen had come into contact the previous day.

'I really *am* sorry,' she began.

The man got awkwardly to his feet and glared at her as she, too, rose. 'Why don't you watch where you're going?' he snapped angrily.

'I said I was — '

'What's the matter with you, anyway? Don't you know how to ski, or something? People like you are a menace on these slopes. You spoil it for everyone else!'

Under his verbal assault, Nicci felt the small measure of confidence she had managed to regain after that business with Peter deserting her. The man was right, of course. Basically untutored in the ways of skiing, she *was* a menace on the slopes. But did he have to be so vindictive about it?

For a moment she considered retreat. It would be a pleasure to get away from this tall, dark-haired stranger with the sour temper. But at the same time she felt she must say something in her own defence.

'I said I was sorry,' she blurted almost before she realised she was speaking. 'I don't know what else I can do. I don't suppose you're entirely blameless yourself. I mean, isn't it supposed to be a golden rule among skiers that they should always be aware of what's going on around them?'

He rolled his eyes to heaven. 'Oh, that's rich! You're a fine one to start spouting 'golden rules' to me. I *was* aware of everything around me, but I've have needed eyes in the back of my *head* to have seen *you* coming!'

Nicci remembered the feeling she'd had about this man the previous day, the idea that he wasn't so much angry at her, but at something else, something against which he was powerless. Staring up at him now, she said, 'It's none of my business, I know, but . . . if it'll make you feel any better, you might just as well go ahead and get it out of your system once and for all.'

That surprised him, silenced him for a moment. His grey eyes mirrored his confusion, then iced over. 'What's that? What do you mean?'

Nicci fought desperately against the urge to turn and flee. Looking him straight in the face, she said, 'It's obvious that *something's* bothering you, and not what's just happened, or that business at the ticket office yesterday — '

He snorted derisively. 'You don't know what you're talking about, woman — '

'Don't I? From the look on your face, I wouldn't be so sure.' She wanted to shut up now. She had said enough, *more* than enough. But it was as if she were on a steam train that just wouldn't stop. 'Look, it's none of my business, and I don't mean to pry, but it strikes me that if you don't get whatever it is out of your system soon, you'll probably explode!'

His eyes blazed furiously as he glowered down at her, and his mouth opened to issue some angry retort. Before he could voice it, however, some of the fire left his eyes, and his broad

shoulders slumped almost impercepti-
bly. 'Woman,' he said in a quieter tone,
'why don't you just get out of my
head?'

Nicci stared up at him with the
oddest feeling in her mind that they
were the only two people on the slope.
She was aware of neither movement
nor sound, only this rugged, worried
stranger. Then the moment passed and
she struggled to pull her eyes away from
his. 'I'm sorry if I was being personal,'
she said, calming down.

'You weren't,' he replied. 'But you
were being perceptive.' For the first
time he smiled, though the smile was
brief and melancholy. 'Are you all
right?'

'Yes.'

'Are you sure? Can you move your
fingers, wiggle your toes?'

'Yes. Please. I'm fine.'

He reached up to cradle her head in
his gloved hands, and peered critically
into her eyes. Again his touch made
her tingle pleasantly, and brought high

colour to her cheeks.

'I'm not a doctor,' he said distantly, 'but I do know a little about first aid, and it's always as well to check for any signs of internal injury.'

She forced a smile to chase away the curious feelings he had awakened in her. 'Will I live?' she asked.

He stepped back. 'Yes.'

'I really *am* sorry about just now.'

'Please, don't be. You were right about what you said. I wasn't concentrating as well as I might have.'

They stood there a moment longer, each feeling a trifle awkward. Then the man said, 'Well, so long as there was no harm done . . . ' And checking the buckles on his boots to make sure his skis were still secure, he took up his poles and began to *shush* away over the slope without a backward glance.

3

Nicci left her skis at the ski-shop and went straight up to her room. Her leg and thigh muscles were aching from all the exercise she'd had throughout the morning, and various other parts of her body were feeling tender as a result of the fall she had taken on the slope.

While she showered, she found herself thinking about the rugged-faced man with whom she'd collided, though she wasn't sure why he should linger in her mind.

Still, he was certainly attractive, and once again she conjured up an image of his grim, preoccupied face, gradually adding detail to the long, weathered countenance.

His grey eyes had held a strange, compelling intensity, she remembered. His nose was straight and sharp, his mouth firm, his teeth white and even, his jawline clearly defined and his skin tanned by long exposure to the Alpine sun.

But there was more to his fascination than mere good looks. There was something *within* him that attracted her and piqued her curiosity. Who was he? She didn't even know his name. Did he live here, in the town? He certainly hadn't struck her as being just another tourist. He had known his way around Zurich, apparently spoke German — and had as good as admitted that something was indeed troubling him.

Although she knew it was none of her business, she wondered what it could possibly be.

The stinging needles of hot water chased away the worst of her aches and pains, and refreshed her. She noticed that her fall had left her with one or two bruises, but apart from a little stiffness, she was in no real discomfort.

Dressing, she went over to the window and peered out across Anderberg, wondering what she should do next. Again her eyes were drawn to the big, square building on the other side of the town, where the mid-afternoon sun bounced brightly off its red bricks and powder blue paintwork, and once more she found herself wondering what the building was.

All the exercise had made her feel pleasantly lazy, and taking the guide-book from Karen's still-unpacked knapsack, she stretched out on her bed to browse. Somewhere along the line, however, she must have dozed off, because the next thing she knew, she was back at work and Peter was confronting her with the petty cash box held in his left hand.

'I need another advance against my expenses,' he said in a harsh and uncompromising tone. 'Give me the key and I'll help myself.'

Nicci felt puzzled. Part of her understood that she was only dreaming, but the rest was confused and uncertain. 'I . . . I haven't got the key,' she replied.

Peter's expression turned savage and he pushed her roughly aside. 'You're lying! Give it to me!'

'I'm not lying!' she replied, although she was. 'The . . . the auditors took it away from me when they found out I'd been letting you help yourself to company funds.'

Peter threw the petty cash box across the room, where it landed with a metallic crash. 'I don't believe you!' he said, his clear blue eyes smouldering with suppressed fury.

'You *have* to,' she insisted, still bluffing.

Peter eyed her sidelong. She knew he was trying to decide whether or not she was telling the truth. Her cheeks felt warm and damp. As he watched her she back-handed the tears away and tried to regain her composure.

Finally Peter said, 'All right. But I still need that money.' He snapped his fingers. '*You* can foot the bill this time.'

And although she shook her head and said no, her purse appeared magically in her hand and she just couldn't help herself; she was giving him everything she had —

'Nicci?'

The voice floated down to her from a great, insurmountable height. In her dream she frowned, trying to identify the speaker. She opened her mouth to ask who was there but her lips were uncooperative and she couldn't voice the question.

'Nicci? Nicci! Are you all right?'

At last she opened her large hazel eyes and blinked a few times. She was on her bed in the room at the Anderberg Hotel, and the sky beyond the window was bathed with a rich, velvety sunset. Karen was perched on the edge of the bed, a frown of concern puckering her brow.

'Nicci?' she said gently.

Nicci cleared her throat and licked her lips. She felt hot and slightly clammy, and her heart was beating rapidly, but she knew where she was now, knew that she'd only been dreaming after all.

Karen got to her feet and stood back

to allow her friend to sit up and swing her legs over the edge of the mattress. 'Are you all right?' she asked again. 'I thought for a moment that you were in pain, the way you were moaning.'

Nicci smiled. 'No pain,' she said. 'Just a dream.'

'A dream?'

'Well, a nightmare, then.'

Karen went over to her own bed, sat down and set about unbuckling her ski boots.

'Have you just come in?' Nicci asked.

'Yes, just this minute.'

'And how was Leno?'

Karen's smile was sheepish. 'Lovely,' she confessed with a girlish giggle. 'He really *does* know his stuff, too. You should see the things he can do on those slopes! I reckon he'd do well in competition, but he says he's not interested. He's always worked in the resorts, and that's how he likes it.'

'I made a friend of my own today,' Nicci said with a laugh, secretly relieved that her dream had been exactly that, and nothing more. 'That fellow we bumped into yesterday.'

'Not Attila the Hun?'

Nicci nodded. 'Yes, that's him. I bumped into him again this afternoon — quite literally, I'm ashamed to say. On my way downslope, I lost control a bit and we collided.'

Karen's mouth dropped open. 'Oh, dear! I bet he really blew his top, didn't he? No wonder you were having nightmares!'

Nicci shook her head, feeling a strange but pleasant flutter of warmth within her as she recalled their encounter. 'Actually, he took it remarkably well — *after* he blew his top, that is. But . . . '

'Yes?'

'I don't know. I can't explain it, really. But I just sense that something's torturing him.'

'It is,' Karen said with a chuckle. 'Us!'

'No, it's more than that. For all his bluster, I get a feeling that he's somehow been worn down by worry. Worn down and almost defeated by it.'

Karen tut-tutted. 'There you go again, analysing people. When will you learn to get on and *enjoy* life instead of looking too deeply into everything?'

Nicci gave no answer, knowing that Karen did not really expect one. They'd had this conversation dozens of times in the past. But Nicci couldn't help the way she was. Oh, she'd been gullible where Peter was concerned, certainly. But more often than not, her natural sensitivity made her receptive to the moods and behaviour of others.

'Leno's invited us out to dinner tonight,' Karen said, changing the subject.

'Us?'

'Yes, you know. You and me. Us.'

Nicci smiled and shook her head. 'I'm sure you won't mind if I cry off.'

'Actually, my girl, I *would* mind. I could use a chaperone to protect me against all that Latin charm. Besides which, we came on this holiday to spend some time *together* — not just so that I could swan off somewhere with the man of my dreams.'

Nicci arched one fine eyebrow. 'Oh, it's as serious as that, is it?' she asked teasingly.

'Well, not *really*,' Karen admitted. Ever the realist, she had no illusions about Leno. They got on well enough, and as far as she was concerned, he was the ideal man with whom to share a holiday romance, but there was nothing more to it than that, and she was quite candid in saying as much.

Nicci was adamant, though. 'Well, I don't suppose Leno will be too upset if I send my regrets,' she remarked. 'Two's company, after all, and the last thing I want to be is a wet blanket.'

'Maybe we could find somebody else and make up a foursome. I'm sure Leno's got a friend who's — '

'Don't give it another thought.'

Karen began to unbutton her ski-suit, but despite the prospect of dinner with Leno, she looked wretched. 'A fine friend I've turned out to be,' she moaned, 'deserting you on our second day here.'

'Well, you're hardly deserting me,' Nicci pointed out. 'Besides, I thought I might take another stroll through the town tonight.'

Karen eyed her sceptically. 'Really?'

'Really,' Nicci replied truthfully. 'I thought I'd make a start on buying postcards and presents for everyone back home.'

Karen chewed her lower lip. 'Well, if you're sure . . . '

'I am. Now go and take a shower. If I know you, it's going to take you forever to decide what you're going to wear tonight.'

Pleased that her friend didn't seem to mind being left alone for the evening, Karen cheered up. 'Hmm. You might have a point there.'

A short while later Nicci slipped into her jacket and set out for her walk through town. Once again the early-evening air was sharp and frosty, but the dark sky was clear and filled with twinkling stars, which meant that there would be no chance of any snow tonight.

As she strolled with her hands stuffed into her pockets, Nicci was reminded that this was the area in which the legendary bowman William Tell was said to have lived, and though Tell was only a product of folklore, the Swiss were very proud of him. Souvenirs depicting both his name and the famous incident when he had proven his marksmanship by shooting an apple off his young son's head were everywhere, as were a seemingly endless display of Swiss cuckoo clocks.

But Nicci enjoyed selecting postcards and making the odd, larger purchase here and there, and found pleasure in walking through the brightly-lit streets with their damp cobblestones, old, mismatched buildings and chattering tourists.

For a while it became easy to forget her troubles, her disturbing nightmare and the reason for having taken this holiday in the first place. Some of the peace of mind she had known out on the slopes that morning returned to ease the worries from her.

Before long she began to feel hungry, and decided to go in search of a café after checking out one last souvenir shop. Its bright, butter-coloured lights drew her inside, and she moved slowly along the shelves to either side in search of gifts to take home with her.

It was whilst browsing that she happened to glance up at an ornate mirror and see the reflection of a tall, blond man in the street outside who so resembled Peter Clark that she gave a small gasp and accidentally dropped the little china ornament she had been deciding whether or not to buy.

The ornament shattered against the tiled floor and Nicci stepped back quickly to avoid the exploding shards of china, giving another, louder gasp. The little old man sitting at the cash register, seeing what had happened, immediately hopped up and came rushing over.

'There iss somesing wrong here?' he asked in heavily-accented English.

Feeling the eyes of the shop's other customers on her, Nicci blushed. 'No, no, I . . . ' She turned to look out into the street. There were plenty of tourists ambling past, but none of them resembled Peter.

With a shuddery sigh, she returned her attention to the irate little shopkeeper. 'I'm terribly sorry,' she said, reaching for her purse. 'I'll pay for the damage, of course.'

'Off course,' the little shopkeeper repeated sternly.

She paid for the shattered ornament with fingers that trembled, and left the shop hurriedly. Outside, the cold evening air cleared her panicky thoughts somewhat. She stood on the pavement and breathed deeply for perhaps half a minute.

After a while she began to calm down, but her thoughts remained unsettled. Why was it that even here, hundreds of miles from home, she couldn't get Peter out of her mind? She didn't love him anymore, she was almost certain. And yet he was constantly in her thoughts.

Then she recalled the nightmare she'd had earlier, and shivered. No, she didn't love Peter anymore, but she thought she understood why he still played such a big part in her life.

It was because she was afraid of him.

She remembered how angry he had become when she had asked him to repay the money he'd taken from the petty cash box, how his voice had deepened, roughened, how his big hands had clenched at his sides, and she realised that, as charming as he might have been, there was also a dark and potentially violent side to his nature.

That was why she couldn't get him out of her mind, then. Because there was always the chance that he might come back into her life, and if she failed to give him whatever he wanted, that dark side of his character would rise to the surface . . .

Her breathing grew shallow and difficult. She wanted only to return to the hotel, shut herself away and calm down. As she turned and started to hurry along the street, however, she walked into someone and, in her agitation, gave another little gasp.

'We meet again,' said the man in front of her.

Because her thoughts were elsewhere, she knew only confusion for a moment. Then she looked up into the face of the rugged man she'd encountered that afternoon on the slopes. Automatically she prepared herself for another argument. 'Oh . . . yes . . . Look, I'm sorry, but — '

Sensing that something was wrong, the man frowned. When he spoke, streams of vapour left his mouth. 'Are you all right?'

The question surprised her. 'Why, yes . . . of course . . . '

'You look a bit shaky to me,' he said with concern.

'No, I'm all right, just . . . just tired, I

71

suppose. It's been a long day . . . '

The man didn't seem totally convinced. 'Even so,' he said, glancing around. He, too, was dressed casually in a padded jacket and grey trousers. 'I'll tell you what. Allow me to buy you a drink at that café over there.'

'Oh, I couldn't — '

'I'd like to. In fact, I think it's the least I can do. I haven't exactly been all that gracious during our last couple of encounters.' He pulled off one glove and offered his hand. 'My name's Thornton, by the way, if you're worried about accepting an invitation to tea from a complete stranger. Andrew Thornton.'

Nicci took his hand and introduced herself. She looked up into his face and was curiously pleased to find him smiling. She could still sense his inner sadness, though, that feeling of hopelessness and defeat that had first aroused her interest in him.

He led her across to a café and they found an empty table over by the steam-beaded window. A waitress came across to them and Andrew eyed Nicci expectantly.

'Oh, just tea, please.'

Andrew ordered for them in German, prompting Nicci to complement him on his knowledge of the language.

'Do you live locally?' she asked.

He nodded. 'Just on the other side of town.' He eyed the bags she'd been carrying. 'You've been shopping, I see. Souvenirs for your loved ones?'

'Yes.'

The tea came with a selection of pastries, and as Andrew spooned sugar into his cup, he fixed her with his intense grey eyes. 'I really *am* sorry about the way I carried on at you yesterday and this afternoon. I'm not usually such a tyrant, I assure you, especially to tourists, who are the life-blood of Anderberg.'

'Don't give it another thought,' Nicci responded, a trifle awkward in his presence, and yet strangely comfortable, too. 'I should apologise to you for what I said earlier. It was wrong of me to make so many personal comments.'

He smiled again, and ran his fingers up through his thick brown hair. 'All we seem to have done since we met is argue and apologise.'

'Well, perhaps we've put all that behind us now.'

'I hope so.'

Nicci took a sip of tea. 'You certainly seem to be a bit more relaxed now than you were this afternoon,' she remarked, keeping her tone light so that he would know she meant no offence. 'Did it help to let off steam a little, as I said it might?'

He shrugged, and that sad look came back into his eyes. 'Not really,' he replied. 'What you see before you now is just a man resigned to his fate. I've fought against it for long enough. I haven't got any more fight left in me.'

Nicci frowned. 'That sounds ominous.'

'Oh, it shouldn't. I don't suppose it will make much difference in the grand scheme of things, but — ' He stopped speaking and took another sip of tea. When he placed his cup back on its saucer, a rueful smile was playing across his lips. 'One last apology,' he said. 'I'm sorry for going on about my own concerns. Now — how are you feeling after our little encounter on the slopes? No broken bones, I'm pleased to see, but one or two bruises, I'll bet.'

'You're right.'

'Yes, it's the same here.' He indicated the pastries. 'Please, help yourself. I ordered them especially.'

Nicci chose a small cake and admitted, 'Today was my first time on skis. Not a very auspicious start, I'm afraid.'

'No,' he agreed, quipping, 'And from here on in, it's all downhill.'

She laughed, and realised with a start that it was the first time she had laughed, *really* laughed, in longer than she could easily recall.

'You're staying up at the Anderberg Hotel, I expect,' he said. 'Most tourists do. It's a nice place.' Suddenly he frowned. 'Where's your friend, by the way?'

'Oh, she's out on a date.'

He showed his surprise. 'My goodness, she must be a fast worker! You only arrived yesterday, didn't you?'

'Well, I don't think it was *all* down to Karen. One of the skiing instructors at the Anderberg had something to do with it, too.'

Andrew's smile was grim. 'Ah, yes, they do. Some of them see young women travelling alone as fair game, I'm afraid.' He caught Nicci's look of alarm and hurried to reassure her. 'Oh, but don't worry. The type of men I'm talking about don't usually last for long in the resorts. The hoteliers just won't tolerate them. If this skiing instructor has been around Anderberg for any length of time — '

'He has, according to what I've heard.'

'There you are, then. Your friend should be in good company.'

'How long have you lived here?' Nicci asked, beginning to warm to the young man on the other side of the table.

'All my life,' he said, 'except for seven years at boarding-school in England, and five years at college. What about yourself? What do you do back home?'

She told him and slowly, as the ice broke, it became somehow easier for them to converse. All her earlier anxiety left her as the minutes stretched into an hour. Peter Clark ceased to become an ogre in her mind. He was just another man, rather like the predatory and unscrupulous skiing instructors Andrew had mentioned earlier on; tolerated by few, rooted out and moved on, never to be allowed back.

At last Nicci glanced around and saw that the café was preparing to close up for the evening, and that they were practically the only customers left. Andrew Thornton suddenly became aware of the fact too, and dug into his pocket for some money with which to settle the bill.

'I didn't mean to detain you for so long,' he said as they rose. 'I hope you don't mind.'

'No, not at all,' she replied. 'It's been very pleasant.'

She reached for her bags, but he beat her to them. 'Here, I'll take those.'

Outside, the street was still quite busy. From one of the *stubli* bars came the sounds of a folk group singing a traditional Swiss ballad, and from the opposite end of the street came the pulsing sounds of music from a disco.

'Are you going back to your hotel now?' Andrew asked.

Nicci nodded. 'Yes. But thank you for the tea, it was very thoughtful.'

'Perhaps you'll allow me to walk you back safely.'

They were standing beneath a sodium streetlight, and she took the opportunity to study his face closely. He had lost some of his worried, preoccupied air, and consequently he looked more his own age than older. But Nicci couldn't really decide why he should want to go to such pains to make up for his earlier hostility. Was it that he really *did* regret all the bitter words they'd exchanged? But why? They were only strangers to each other, nothing more. Or was it that —

No, it was an uncharitable thought, and she hated herself for thinking it. But . . . was it possible that he was one of the very men he had warned her about earlier, one who saw women travelling alone as 'fair game'?

The thought made her feel uneasy. He had seemed so plausible back in the café, but then he *would*, wouldn't he? And in any case, what did she really know about him? Oh, he'd said a fair bit throughout the course of the evening, yes, but now that she thought about it, everything had been vague, nothing specific.

'Uh, that's all right, Andrew,' she said stiffly. 'There's no need for that.'

For just an instant he appeared crestfallen, but then he forced a smile onto his rugged face and nodded. 'Well, at least let me see you to the bus-stop. The service gets notoriously unreliable as the evening wears on.'

'That's all right, I was going to walk anyway.'

He looked her straight in the face, but she refused to meet his eyes. Sensing the sudden chill in her mood, he nodded again, more slowly this time, and handed over her bags. 'Well, take care then, Nicci. Thank you for this evening. It wasn't much, I know, but I enjoyed it a great deal.'

He turned and strode off down the street, hands jammed into his pockets, shoes clicking rhythmically against the cobblestones.

Nicci watched him go, feeling despondent. She hadn't meant to hurt his feelings, and if he had taken her reluctance as a lack of interest, he was certainly wrong. Andrew Thornton interested her greatly, and though she tried to deny it, the attraction she felt for him was both strong and profound.

But she had no desire to give her

heart to another man who might abuse it and then break it the same way Peter had, and she had to concede that maybe she'd been wise to back away from him before their relationship really got the chance to blossom.

Slowly her own feeling of euphoria began to dissipate. She realised that she'd been foolish to even *consider* starting a relationship with a man she would only know for a fortnight, and never see again after that.

With a sigh she made her way back through the streets and up to the hotel, which fairly blazed with light.

Despite the fact that she'd slept for a time earlier that afternoon, she was beginning to feel tired again by the time she entered the bustling hotel reception and started across towards the desk to collect her room key. It had, after all, been a long and eventful day, and the muscles in her legs and thighs were starting to ache again. The prospect of another shower and then a good night's rest held great appeal for her.

It was just as she was carrying her purchases from the desk to the elevators that someone called her name from the doorway leading into the combination bar and lounge, and expecting to find Karen and Leno coming out to greet her, she turned and switched on a welcoming smile.

The smile, however, died on her lips.

'Hello, Nicci,' said the man in the doorway. 'Long time no see.'

For a moment Nicci fought to overcome a wave of nausea and giddiness. She felt all the colour drain from her face, but somehow she regained control of herself, although that control was tenuous, to say the least.

'P — Peter!' she husked, disbelief plain in her voice. 'What . . . what on earth are *you* doing here?'

4

For a moment Nicci just stood there, unable to believe her eyes. How *could* Peter be here? It was impossible . . . wasn't it?

But then he reached up and brushed his fine blond hair back off his forehead, and the gesture was so much a part of him that she knew beyond any shadow of doubt that her imagination wasn't playing tricks on her at all. He really *was* here.

'What . . . what *are* you doing here?' she repeated in a cracked, stunned whisper.

Behind her the light above one of the elevators came on and the doors slid smoothly apart. Without batting an eyelid, Peter took her by one arm and led her inside. 'What floor are you on?' he asked.

She glared at him for a moment, until

his infuriating, winning smile made her look away.

'Don't look so concerned,' he said pleasantly. 'I'm not out to abduct you.'

Nicci fought to bring her breathing under control. When she felt that she was over the worst of the shock and more in control of herself, she answered him and he pressed one of the buttons.

The doors slid shut.

As the elevator began to rise, she knew a moment of claustrophobia, and stifled the urge to panic. She was realizing one of her strongest fears, being alone with the very man who had humiliated, and now haunted, her. But she knew that under no circumstances must she show that fear.

'To answer your question,' he said, regarding her through the cool blue eyes she remembered so well, 'I'm here on honeymoon.'

Nicci glanced up at him sharply, surprise conquering her fear. 'Honey — !' She treated him to a withering, disdainful look. 'Doesn't your wife think it a bit strange that you should suddenly disappear with another woman?'

His winning smile stayed intact. He was as tall and athletic as she remembered, and equally as smart in a blue blazer over a white shirt and grey slacks. 'She's off powdering her nose,' he replied. 'Otherwise I wouldn't have dared to come out and call to you.'

Nicci made no reply to that, but her lips thinned down as she felt his hot gaze rake her skin.

'You haven't changed a bit,' he said appreciatively. 'Still as gorgeous as ever.'

'Oh, don't be fooled, Peter,' she told him. 'I've changed, all right. Inside.'

At last his confidence faltered a bit and he assumed a look of contrition. 'Look, I know we didn't really have much of a chance to talk . . . towards the end, I mean . . . But you know you meant a lot to me, Nicci. A hell of a lot.'

The hand gripping her arm relaxed slightly, and the fingers began to move slowly in a soft, gentle caress. But Nicci found contact with him somehow obscene, and quickly shrugged out of his grasp.

'What I meant to you,' she said, this time meeting his gaze, 'was precisely one hundred pounds.'

He regarded her blankly. 'Eh?'

He didn't even *remember* the incidents with the petty cash money, then! That was how much it had meant to him.

He switched his smile back on and brushed his hair back off his forehead again. In the confines of the elevator the smell of his aftershave was rich and unpleasant, and Nicci marvelled at how she could ever have found such a repulsive man so attractive.

At last the elevator came to a halt and the doors whispered open. Nicci hurried out into the quiet, empty corridor and Peter followed her, reaching out to take hold of one of her hands before she could rush away and leave him standing there alone.

'Hang on a minute,' he said, sobering. 'What I really want to say to you won't take long, I promise.'

Nicci stared up at him. His tone and expression made her decide to give him the benefit of the doubt. She wondered if, beneath his brash, urbane exterior, he too regretted their relationship, and the way it had ended. Perhaps she had misjudged him. Perhaps he wanted to offer an apology and end things on a less hostile note. If indeed that *was* the case, it would be wrong of her to deny him the opportunity.

'All right,' she said, still finding it hard to believe that she was having this conversation. 'I'm listening.'

He appeared relieved. 'Will you be staying in Anderberg for long?'

'A fortnight. We only arrived yesterday.'

'We?'

'Yes. Karen Payne and I. You remember Karen.'

His relief turned to discomfort. 'Well,' he said in a low but earnest voice, 'I'd like to ask you a favour.'

She blinked. 'A favour?'

'Yes. You see, Rachel — she's my wife

— Rachel's a lovely girl, but she does have one fault. She's very jealous of me. If she knew I was here talking to you now, she'd throw a fit. So . . . ' He paused and licked his lips. 'So, if you should see me around the hotel any time within the next fortnight, be a love and walk right by as if you don't know me. All right?'

Nicci's hazel eyes narrowed at the nerve of the man. Not one word of apology for all his lies and deceit, not one word of thanks for all the covering up she'd done for him with the expense money . . . Instead he was only concerned with his own image.

She shook her head slowly in disgust, feeling emotion well up inside her at this man whose thoughts had only ever been for himself.

'It should be easy to ignore you, Peter,' she said in a tone that surprised him. 'Because I *don't* know you, not really. I don't know you at *all*.'

★ ★ ★

Karen got back to their darkened hotel room sometime after midnight. She closed the door quietly behind her and let her breath out in a heavy, contented sigh.

'Forget everything I said earlier,' she announced to the shadowy figure lying in the bed nearest to the window. 'I *am* in love with that great big Italian hunk. He's tall, he's dark, he's handsome, and what's more, he thinks I'm the greatest thing since sliced bread. What more could I ask of a man, pray tell?'

She moved carefully around the furniture and sat on the edge of her own bed, then reached up to unclip her ear-rings. 'Did or did I not tell you I should have taken you along as a chaperone?' she asked, slurring her words ever so slightly. 'As it was, I was completely defenceless against Leno's Latin charm.'

She kicked her shoes off and squinted across at the indistinct, motionless shape of her friend. 'Nicci? Are you awake, or am I talking to myself again?'

At first there was no response, and Karen assumed that Nicci was asleep. But then Nicci turned over with a soft rustle of cotton and looked at the other girl without saying a word, and that was when Karen knew that something was wrong.

'Nic?' she said in a half-whisper. 'What is it? What's happened?'

In the darkness, Nicci cleared her throat. 'It's Peter,' she said in a small, wretched voice. 'He . . . he's here.'

Karen's frown deepened. '*What*?'

Reaching over, she switched on the lamp that sat on the table between the two beds, flooding the room with warm yellow light. 'What's that you — '

She fell silent as she saw Nicci's moist, bloodshot eyes. Even as she watched, fresh tears began to slide like melting pearls down her smooth, pale cheeks. At once Karen's heart went out to her.

'Oh, Nic . . . '

She went to her friend with open arms and before she could properly gather her up in a supportive embrace, Nicci's slim frame began to shudder with a series of heart-breaking sobs.

'He . . . he's here,' she repeated. 'You know, I . . . I thought I saw him last night . . . when . . . when we were at that *stubli* bar . . . and . . . and again, earlier, while I was looking around one of the souvenir shops . . . but . . . but I thought it was my imagination.'

Karen's voice was grim and protective, all hint of her previous high spirits now gone. 'Did he say what he was doing here?'

'He's on honeymoon . . . '

'You're kidding!'

Nicci reached for a tissue, blew her nose and dabbed at her eyes. She hadn't meant to cry, she didn't want to give Peter the satisfaction, but once she'd reached the safety of their room, all the events of the past few months had boiled to the surface and she'd been unable to stop herself. After a while she'd thought she'd got it out of her system, but then, when Karen had come in and she'd tried to tell her what had happened, the unfairness of it all had overwhelmed her again.

Now, however, she felt that the worst was behind her. Karen sat back, her own perfect blue eyes moist and her bottom lip quivering dangerously.

'What did he say?' the blonde girl asked softly.

'That his wife was jealous of him,' Nicci replied, calmer now. 'And that if I were to see him around the hotel at all, I was to pretend that I didn't know him.'

Karen gave a derisive snort. 'What, and that was all? Nothing else? No apologies or — '

'No, nothing else.'

'The lousy little rat! My God, no wonder he doesn't want to upset his wife! It's her father who's paying his wages, isn't it!' She stood up, indignant and vengeful. 'Pretend we don't know him?' she repeated. 'Under any other circumstances, it would be a pleasure. But no way am I going to let him get away with treating you so badly. If you ask me, it's about time somebody told his jealous wife a few home truths.'

'Leave it, Kar.'

'*What?*'

Nicci's voice was tired. 'Leave it. There's nothing to be gained by stirring up any more trouble.'

Karen stared down at her. She was going to argue the point, Nicci could tell, but then she thought better of it. 'All right,' she said. 'If that's what you want.'

'It is. But . . . '

'What?'

'I can't stay in the same hotel with him,' Nicci confessed grimly. 'It makes my skin crawl just to *think* that I might bump into him.'

Karen took that in and considered the alternatives. 'What do you suggest we do, then? Find another hotel?'

'Well, that would be the best thing. But I can't expect you to leave the Anderberg. For one thing, we won't get a refund on the money we paid to stay here, and I don't think it's fair that you should lose out on that because of me. And for another thing . . . '

'Go on.'

'Well, there's Leno to consider.'

'Oh . . . '

Nicci's smile was weary. 'You've obviously grown quite attached to him. It would be a shame if you couldn't go on seeing him for as long as we're here.'

'Oh . . . poppycock! We came on this holiday together, Karen and Nicci, the Terrible Twosome! If you think I'm going to let you go off on your own, you can forget it.'

'I won't be going off on my own,' Nicci replied calmly. 'We'll still be sharing the holiday together. The only difference is, we'll be staying at separate hotels.' She made a brave attempt to cheer up. 'I thought you'd be pleased at the prospect of having the room to yourself. Besides . . . '

Karen saw the look on her face and said, 'What?'

Nicci released a shuddery sigh. 'I've

already had a word with the manager. I've settled my part of the bill and I'll be checking out in the morning.'

Karen was incredulous. '*What*?'

'First thing tomorrow,' Nicci informed her sadly, 'I'm booking into a place called the Rose, on the other side of town.'

★　★　★

Next morning, following a sleepless night, Nicci showered and dressed in the early stillness, then packed her things back into her knapsack and small case. She had decided last night that she would be leaving first thing today. She didn't want to take even the remotest chance of seeing Peter again.

Sitting at the dressing-table, she slowly brushed her wavy auburn hair and regarded herself in the mirror. It was ironic, she thought. She had taken this holiday in order to mend her broken heart and rebuild her ailing confidence. Instead the entire fortnight looked as if it might turn into one big disaster.

'You're not going already?'

Nicci shifted her eyeline so that she could see Karen's reflection as she slowly sat up in bed. Karen's blonde hair was awry and her eyes were narrowed and sleepy, but there was also a sad, downward curve to her lips.

Nicci nodded. 'Yes. I thought I'd make an early start.'

Karen stifled a yawn. 'Hang on a minute, then, and I'll come with you, see you settled in okay.'

Nicci gave a short chuckle, trying to assure her friend that she was all right, and didn't really mind having to move to another hotel in the slightest. 'Stay where you are,' she said. 'Not that I believe you could get out of that bed even if you wanted to.'

Karen placed a palm on her forehead. 'Are you incinerating that I can't hold my drink?' she asked, going cross-eyed and deliberately mis-pronouncing her words.

Nicci's laugh came more naturally this time, and she felt a great affection well up in her for this girl who always cheered her up, no matter how life wore her down. She stood up and went over to her.

'Go back to sleep,' she said fondly. 'I'm a big girl now. I'm sure I can find my way to the Rose Hotel in one piece.'

Karen looked up at her. 'Will you be all right, though?' she asked seriously.

'Of course. I'll tell you what; why don't you pop over to see me later on? I can show you my room, might even buy you lunch, and then we'll take a hike along those footpaths on the far side of town.'

'I'll certainly pop over,' Karen replied, stifling another jaw-cracking yawn. 'I'll let you buy me lunch, too. But I can't promise to get all energetic and go for a long walk.'

'Fair enough.' Nicci looked into her friend's eyes, and their mood sobered abruptly. 'See you later, then.'

Gathering up her baggage, Nicci left the room.

Outside, the early morning was quiet

and chilly. Somewhere nearby, someone was baking bread, and Nicci savoured its fresh, appetizing aroma.

She was feeling a bit apprehensive now, because although she hadn't said as much to Karen, the comments the Anderberg's manager had made about the Rose Hotel last night had been less than complimentary. 'There are, off course, several guest houses in the town, but thiss far into the season, I doubt that you would find a room,' he had pointed out in brisk, German-laced English. 'There are alwayss roomss at the Rose Hotel, however. It is, not really too much in demand these days, antiquated, you know, somesing of a dinosaur compared to the Anderberg.'

Now Nicci wondered what unpleasantries still lay in store for her.

It would take quite a while to walk through to the other side of town, and her progress would be considerably hampered by her knapsack and case, so she decided to make the journey by bus. After a ten-minute wait, one of the bright yellow vehicles arrived and she climbed aboard and named her destination.

The journey didn't take long, although there were frequent stops to take on more passengers along the way. A quarter of an hour later, the bus driver twisted around, smiled at her and said, 'Rose Hotel?'

Nicci scooped up her luggage and stepped down from the bus. 'Thank you,' she said with a grateful nod. '*Danke.*'

As the bus pulled away, Nicci saw that she was standing just across the road from the square, red-brick building which had so commanded her attention from the window of her old room back at the Anderberg. At first she thought there must have been some mistake, but according to the sign above the elegant, if old-fashioned, double doors, this was indeed her destination.

She looked up at the grand structure. She was relieved to see that it didn't look as bad as the Anderberg's manager had made out, at least not from outside. It still remained to be seen what the rooms and service were like, however.

Crossing the narrow, deserted road, she climbed the steps to the double doors and went inside.

It was almost like stepping back in time. The reception was small and cosy. A sofa and some potted plants ran along one wall. Just above a ticking radiator was an old framed picture of the Rose Hotel in its heyday. Straight ahead was a wide staircase, beside a single, pine-panelled elevator, and to Nicci's right was the registration desk, empty at the moment.

Nicci went across to the desk and set down her things. All around her the hotel was silent, save for an odd, indistinct sound filtering downstairs from above that sounded like a child's laughter.

Nicci glanced around, hoping that someone would appear through the door on the other side of the registration desk and break the funereal hush with a smile and a greeting, but no-one did.

Finally she decided to ring the highly-polished brass bell beside the register. It sang out musically, loud in the silence. No-one came to answer it immediately, but she did hear someone moving around in the room beyond the door.

At last she heard footsteps hurrying across the floor, and then a man appeared in the doorway. 'Good morning, I'm sorry to have kept you . . . Nicci!'

Nicci was as surprised to see Andrew Thornton as he was to see her. But mingled with her surprise was a wonderful sense of tranquillity, a peculiar but not unpleasant feeling of 'coming home'. He was, after all, a friendly face, and if ever she needed a friendly face, it was now.

'Well, this *is* a surprise,' he said, recovering himself and offering her a smile of welcome. Suddenly, however, he frowned. 'Is everything all right?'

She nodded. 'Yes. But I'd like a room if you've got one.'

'Oh, I've got plenty. But I thought you were staying at the Anderberg?'

'I was,' she replied, not meeting his curious stare. 'But ... something personal happened. I ... I thought it would be better to move to another hotel.'

Andrew's expression was sympathetic. 'You haven't had an argument with your friend, I hope.'

'Oh, no, nothing like that.'

He nodded. 'I understand.' It was obvious that he didn't, but to his credit, he made no further attempt to uncover the truth.

He opened the register and checked the availability of the rooms. He was wearing a crisp white shirt, dark grey trousers and a wine-red tie this morning, and he looked very business-like. 'What sort of room would you like?' he asked. 'We've plenty to choose from.' He looked up at her, and she couldn't help but notice the smoky grey quality of his eyes. 'Do you have any preference?'

'No preference,' she replied. 'Anything cheap and cheerful will do.'

He wasn't sure if she were joking. 'Really?'

Her expression was sheepish. 'I didn't plan on having to pay out for two lots of accommodation, so as of this morning, I'm running on a limited budget.' She forced a smile to take away some of the seriousness of her plight.

'All right,' he said, 'let's see what we can do for you . . . ' He studied the register a moment longer, then reached a decision. 'The Rose Room should suit you, I think. I daresay we could probably offer you a special rate for what's left of your fortnight, too.'

'Oh, no. I couldn't — '

'Nonsense.'

'But you can't just make up special rates to suit yourself, Andrew! You'll get in trouble with the manager!'

He chuckled. 'I *am* the manager,' he said. 'I own this place.'

'*Own* it — !'

He turned the register around and offered her a pen. 'Now, let's hear no more about it,' he said firmly. While she signed in, he took down a key and came around the desk to pick up her luggage. 'All set?'

She nodded.

'Come on, then, this way.'

Ignoring the elevator, he began to ascend the stairs, and Nicci fell in alongside him. 'You'll have to make allowances for us,' he explained apologetically. 'The Rose is a bit old-fashioned, and since I only employ one member of staff, the service tends to be slow, but the rooms are spacious and comfortable, and *Frau* Blucher is a marvellous cook.'

Nicci, still amazed by this new turn of events, thought she understood now why Andrew had always seemed to be worried and preoccupied. Running such a large hotel practically single-handed must be an awesome responsibility. 'I imagine you have your work cut out for you,' she remarked.

He shook his head. 'I only wish I did. But when you've only got a handful of guests, the place more or less runs itself.'

She caught the sorrow in his voice, and although he tried to mask it, she heard the bitterness, too.

They reached the second floor and Andrew led her along a wide, richly-carpeted corridor. Nicci was impressed with the hotel. It held an elegance and style that the Anderberg lacked, and she was unable to understand why bookings should be low.

'Ah, here we are,' he said, coming to a halt before one ornately-finished door. Unlocking it, he swung the portal wide and ushered her into a large room decorated with a selection of sturdy pine furniture and a wide, four-poster bed. Sunlight streamed in through the thick lace curtains at the windows to land in bright, cheery puddles on the thick grey carpet and the lavender walls.

'Good grief!' Nicci breathed, unprepared

for such luxury. 'Andrew . . . this room, it's . . . well, I've never seen anything like it! It's so *grand*!'

'I thought you'd like it,' he said, pleased by her reaction. 'It was always my mother's favourite, too. In fact, the hotel, and this room, were named after her.'

A new thought occurred to Nicci. 'Oh, but . . . I couldn't afford it.' She blushed. 'Really. Do you have something cheaper?'

'I thought we'd settled all that.'

'But I can't accept charity — '

'It isn't charity. Call it, I don't know . . . ' He shrugged. 'A closing down offer.'

His words stunned her, and she frowned at him. 'Closing down? Are you joking, Andrew?'

He shook his head, his eyes full of pain now, and his jaw set firm. 'I wish I were,' he replied. 'But the sad truth is that we're only going through the motions now, until the season ends in April. After that the Rose closes its doors for the last time, I'm afraid.'

The news stung her more deeply than she could have imagined. It seemed somehow criminal to close such a magnificent hotel, like tearing a page out of history.

She went over to him, understanding now exactly why he had been in such a foul mood when she'd first met him, understanding also what he'd meant when he'd told her he was a man resigned to his fate, a man who had fought against the inevitable long enough, and had no more fight left in him.

'Is it your location, here in Anderberg?' she asked gently. 'Is that why business has tailed off?'

He shrugged. 'Yes — and no,' he answered tiredly. 'In many respects, the Rose is a victim of Anderberg's success. There's just too much competition, you see. The Anderberg Hotel takes four times as many tourists as we could, and they offer so many modern conveniences, as you're no doubt aware. The skiing is ideal over there, too, whereas most of the slopes behind the Rose are too thickly-forested to allow for safe skiing. They're ideal for hikers, but that's about all.'

'And that's why people have stopped coming to the Rose?'

He nodded. 'More or less. Oh, it hasn't just happened overnight. It's been a gradual process. When my parents ran the place, we could always guarantee to be packed to capacity. When they died, I took over things, and for a while business carried on as before. But then the Anderberg sprang up, and the guest houses began to tout more aggressively for a slice of the tourist trade.'

'Couldn't you try to upgrade the Rose?' she suggested, adding truthfully, 'Not that I think it needs it.'

'Upgrading takes money, Nicci, and the banks will only invest if they have confidence in the end results.' His smile was brief. 'That's where I'd been the other day, when I first ran into you at Kloten Airport; seeing my bank manager to make one last, unsuccessful appeal for cash.'

She tried to cheer him up. 'No wonder you were in such a bad mood. It sounds as if you had good reason.'

'If I could only have made it through this season with a modest profit to show for my efforts,' he said, speaking more to himself than to Nicci. 'The bank might have been a bit more sympathetic, then.' He sighed expressively. 'You know, I thought all my worries were over when I landed a booking for two separate parties of school-children coming out from England on a skiing trip a month or so ago. They would have given me just the profit I needed to carry on. But do you see what's happened? We've had no snow here for months, and I've never had cash enough to install an artificial run on our one good slope.'

'Have you lost the bookings?'

'Not yet, but it's only a matter of time, unless we have a miracle sometime within the next couple of weeks.'

'I'm sorry, Andrew.'

He smiled, returning his gaze to her.

'There we go again, apologising.'

'Yes,' she said. 'But at least it's not because we've had another argument, this time.'

Their eyes met and once more she had the strangest feeling that nobody else existed, just she and Andrew. So entranced did she become by him that she almost forgot to breathe.

At last she said, 'I wish there was something I could do to help you.'

'There is,' he replied, crossing over to the door. 'Pray, Nicci. Pray for snow.'

5

When Karen came over later that day, she was both impressed and envious.

'You jammy devil!' she said, finishing her inspection of the Rose Room and its adjoining bath suite. 'No wonder you were in such a hurry to leave the Anderberg! You must have known what you'd be coming to!'

She sat on the edge of the four-poster bed and bounced up and down for a moment or so to test the mattress. 'Hey, you know, I might well move out of the Anderberg myself, if I know I'm going to get a room like this.'

Nicci, over by one of the windows, smiled teasingly. 'What, and desert poor Leno?'

Karen considered that. 'Hmmm. That's a point. A palace without a prince isn't really a palace at all, is it?'

'Who says this palace hasn't got a prince?'

Karen regarded her sidelong. 'You're not talking about Attila the Hun, surely?'

'Well, he's certainly good-looking, and he's a gentleman right down to his fingertips. Oh, I know we all got off on the wrong foot, but . . . ' She trailed off, suddenly embarrassed.

Karen wasn't about to let her off so easily, though. 'Don't tell me you've gone all soft over him?' she said with her customary directness.

'Of course not,' Nicci replied hurriedly, although she wasn't at all certain that she was being completely honest. 'But he's been very kind to me, especially at a time when he's got such worrying problems of his own.'

Karen's blue eyes shone with mischief. 'Well, I hope you'll both be very happy together.'

Feeling herself blush, Nicci went in search of a topic with which she might change the subject. 'Have you run into Peter for yourself, yet?'

Karen grew serious, too. 'Yes. At

breakfast this morning, him *and* his precious wife. You should have seen him, feeding his face as if he didn't have a care in the world . . . '

'The rat,' Nicci said, using the insult before Karen could. 'You, ah . . . you didn't say anything to either of them . . . did you?'

'No. But don't think I didn't want to.'

Nicci was relieved. 'Anyway, enough of this idle chatter. I'd buy you lunch, but they only do breakfasts and evening meals here. Do you fancy a sandwich instead?'

Karen rolled her eyes to heaven. 'Oh, you *do* spoil me,' she said with a laugh, secretly glad to see that her friend had perked up so since this morning. 'All right, Nic; if you're going to treat me, I'd be a fool to say no — even if it *is* only to a measly sandwich!'

★   ★   ★

Over their snack-lunch in a small, flower-filled park not too far from the

113

centre of town, Karen confessed that Leno had asked her out to dinner again that evening, but that she had said no.

'What on earth for?' asked Nicci.

Her blonde friend looked awkward. 'Well, it's just not right. I mean, ever since we've been here, we've hardly spent any time together.'

'Of course we have! In case you've forgotten, I'm still aching from all the hours we put in on those slopes yesterday. And we've been together today.' Nicci turned to Karen. They were sitting on a bench to one side of a neat gravel pathway. 'If Leno likes you enough to want to take you out again, you'd be a fool to say no.'

Karen shrugged. 'It just doesn't seem right, though.'

'I don't know why. *I* don't mind in the least. As far as I'm concerned, good luck to you.'

'But what will *you* be doing while I'm off gallivanting? It can't be much fun trying to make your own amusements all alone in a strange town.'

'Oh, I don't know,' Nicci said with a great show of nonchalance. 'I've got my prince to keep me occupied, haven't I?'

Karen grinned. 'That's right, I'd forgotten about him . . . Nic, what are you looking at?'

Nicci took her eyes off the few clouds above. 'Oh, I was just wondering what's happened to all the snow.'

'You remember what Leno said — he says there isn't going to *be* any this year.'

'Well, I hope he's wrong, for Andrew's sake.' She cast a brief glance at her friend's profile. 'So — it's settled then, is it? You'll take Leno up on his invitation tonight after all?'

Karen showed reluctance. 'I still don't think it's very fair on you . . . '

'Let *me* be the judge of that.'

'Well . . . all right, then.'

They spent the rest of the afternoon window-shopping, then split up as the sun began to sink, each to go back to their separate hotels with a promise to meet again the following day.

How peculiar this holiday was turning out to be, though, Nicci thought as she walked back through the picturesque streets. They'd only been here for two days, and yet so much had happened.

Most curious of all, however, was Nicci's attitude. Far from feeling low and dejected after having run into Peter Clark, she didn't believe she had ever felt happier.

Perhaps the clean Swiss air agreed with her — or perhaps it was because she was returning to the Rose Hotel, and Andrew Thornton.

★   ★   ★

Andrew was certainly right about his one employee, *Frau* Blucher. She was the most accomplished of cooks, and over a sumptuous meal of veal in cream sauce, Nicci got her first good look at her fellow guests.

There were, as Andrew had told her earlier, only a handful. Two young

116

students sat in one corner, conversing quietly over laden platters. An elderly gentleman was reading a French newspaper whilst eating, and a married couple in their thirties were trying to control their two young children, who kept regarding Nicci curiously through the backs of their chairs.

After a while, one of the children, a fair-haired eight-year-old boy, slipped down from his chair and walked over. 'Hello,' he said with a shy smile.

Nicci pushed her plate aside and smiled back at him. 'Hello. I'm Nicci. What's your name?'

'David Blake.'

David Blake's mother caught Nicci's eye and offered an apology. 'I'm sorry about the interruption,' she said in a long-suffering tone. 'David — come back here at once!'

'Don't worry,' Nicci told her understandingly. 'He's no trouble. In fact, he's keeping me company while I eat, aren't you, David?'

David nodded shyly, climbing onto a

chair opposite her.

'You're sure he's no bother?' the boy's mother asked.

'Of course not.'

At that point, David's six-year-old sister came over and struggled up onto a chair beside Nicci. She too had fair hair and the clear, fascinated gaze that all children possess.

'It looks like you've made yourself a couple of friends,' the children's father remarked with a laugh. 'But send them back if they become a handful.'

David and his sister Jennifer proved to be well-behaved and polite, however. 'I want to be a mountaineer when I grow up,' David announced importantly. 'What do you want to be?'

Nicci smiled affectionately at her young companions. 'Oh, I don't know . . . A fairy princess.'

'Me too!' squealed Jennifer. 'A fairy princess *and* a mountaineer.'

A short while later Andrew appeared in the dining room doorway, and sighting her, came over. 'Well, you're certainly proving to be popular with the younger generation,' he said, crouching down to put himself on the same level as the children. 'David and Jennifer here didn't want to know me, did you?'

The children avoided his gaze, suddenly going coy. A moment later, as if by mutual consent, they slipped down off their chairs and skipped back over to their parents.

Andrew watched them go, then turned his attention back to Nicci. 'You see — the story of my life. I scare everyone away.'

'You haven't scared me,' Nicci pointed out as he took the chair David had just vacated.

'No, but I did, very nearly, a few days ago.'

That was true, although it seemed hard to believe that she'd only known him for such a short length of time. Thinking back, initially to their first encounter at the airport, and their second on the slopes behind the Anderberg, it amazed her that their friendship should ever have flourished at all.

'Well,' he said, breaking in on her thoughts. 'If you'll excuse me, I've got some paperwork to finish before bed-time, and I *must* help Frau Blucher with the washing-up, otherwise she'll throw a tantrum.'

'Could *I* help at all?' Nicci asked on impulse. 'I mean, I'd like to. And it's the very least I can do in return for all your generosity.'

'I wouldn't hear of it,' he replied firmly. 'You're a guest here, after all. And I have the reputation of the Rose Hotel to uphold . . . at least until the end of April, that is.'

★　★　★

The following morning Nicci awoke from the first really settled sleep she'd known for a long time, and after bathing, dressed and went downstairs.

It was still fairly early, and the grand hotel was quiet and peaceful. In the reception, however, it was a completely different story. Andrew was speaking in fluent German to a laundryman whose van was parked outside.

Judging from the dusters and polish on the reception desk, and the vacuum cleaner which had been left to one side of the staircase, it looked as if the laundry man's visit had interrupted Andrew's attempt to clean up. Now the grey-eyed hotelier was gesturing with his hands to indicate that the laundry-man should take his van around to the back of the Rose to unload.

After a moment Andrew noticed Nicci standing on the staircase watching him. 'Excuse me just a moment,' he told her wearily. Addressing the laundry man again, he said, 'Look, come with me and I'll *show* you where to go.'

Together the two men went out into the street and Andrew got into the van beside the driver. As he gave directions in German, the driver started the engine and drove the van out of sight.

Nicci came down the rest of the stairs

and stood a moment in the empty reception. She'd meant what she'd said the previous evening about wanting to help out, and this seemed like a good opportunity to do just that. But would she offend Andrew? They said the road to hell was paved with good intentions, but . . .

On impulse, Nicci went over to the desk and selected the cleaning implements she would need. Then she set about dusting the reception.

It was hardly a glamorous task, and certainly no job to be doing whilst on holiday, but she found the work oddly satisfying, as if she were somehow according the elegant building the respect it deserved. By the time she began to vacuum the carpet, the woodwork held a rich shine, and the brass bell gleamed brightly.

It was as she was sweeping down the front steps that a shadow suddenly fell across her, and she looked up to see Peter Clark's broad, confident smile.

'What's all this, then? Taken on a part-time cleaning job now, have you?'

he asked, brushing his hair back off his forehead.

As soon as her initial jolt of surprise wore off, Nicci regarded him coolly, no longer as afraid of him as she had been.

'Hey, you didn't have to move out of the Anderberg, you know,' he said generously when she made no reply to his original statement. 'I mean, I know it upset you to see me here, that was obvious, but I didn't think you'd go running off to a nunnery.'

'This isn't a nunnery,' she said quietly. 'It happens to be a very beautiful hotel.'

Peter glanced up at the building. 'If you say so,' he said without much interest. 'Listen, Nicci . . . I don't want us to be enemies any more than I think you do. Can't we call a truce?'

'I don't know,' Nicci responded. 'Can we?'

'Look, Rachel's taking one of those blasted coaches to the Oberalp Pass today. She's dead keen on skiing, a bit of a purist, prefers real snow to the dry slopes . . . so I'm at a bit of a loose end.'

Nicci could hardly believe her ears. Surely he wasn't going to ask her out on a date! Even Peter must have *some* principles, she thought. But evidently he didn't, as his next words revealed.

'How do you fancy going to the ice rink with me this afternoon? We could patch up our differences, have a few laughs. It'd be like the old days . . . '

Nicci shook her head, clearly scandalised. 'Peter, you're a married man! Good grief — this is supposed to be your honeymoon!'

His response was only a casual shrug. 'So? What the eye doesn't see . . . '

'You,' she said with a curl of the lip, 'are disgusting.'

That jarred the smile from his face. His blue eyes iced over and he brushed his fine blond hair back off his forehead again, very slowly.

'You'll be sorry you said that,' he muttered, taking a threatening step closer.

'I don't think so,' said a new voice.

Peter and Nicci both wheeled around to find Andrew standing on the narrow pavement behind them. He wore a grave look as he glowered in Peter's direction, and Peter was clearly intimidated by him.

'Now, I don't know what all this is about,' Andrew told him quietly, 'and I don't *want* to know. It's personal, and it's between the two of you. But if I ever hear you threaten this girl again, so help me . . . '

Peter backed off. 'All right, all right, no need for any unpleasantness . . . '

He spun on his heel and stalked away.

Andrew released a heavy sigh, but he didn't relax. Nicci, looking up at him, couldn't say for sure, but she thought she caught a hint of jealousy in his smoky grey eyes. But that couldn't be . . . could it?

He cleared his throat. 'I'm sorry if you thought I was interfering,' he began.

'I didn't. In fact, I can't tell you how

glad I was to see you standing there.'

He smiled briefly, obviously pleased by what she'd said. 'I'm *not* prying, but . . . was *he* your reason for leaving the Anderberg?'

She nodded. 'Yes. I used to know him.'

'Long ago?'

'Actually, it's not that long, but it seems like a lifetime.' A smile touched her full lips. 'Believe it or not, he's here on honeymoon.'

'What, and he's still pestering you?'

'Yes. But I doubt that he'll do it any more, not now that you've warned him off.'

He shrugged, attempting to make light of it. 'Well, just call that my good deed of the day.'

They went back into the reception and he noticed at once how clean everything looked. 'Talking of good deeds . . . ' he said.

'I hope you didn't mind, but I wanted to do something to repay all your kindness.'

He looked down at her, and his

expression grew very serious. They were standing face to face, so close that she could feel the heat of his body coming through his open-necked shirt in clean-smelling waves.

'You know,' he said, 'I think your coming to Anderberg was the best thing that's ever happened to me.'

She wanted to reach up and kiss him, and she could tell that he felt the same way about her. But the knowledge frightened her. This wasn't love, it was just her own silly idea of a holiday romance, wasn't it?

Suddenly Nicci felt her heart racing faster, and she knew she must not encourage the emotions she felt certain they were both experiencing. She took a pace away from him, breaking the spell that bound them together, and said, 'I've been thinking . . . about your problems here at the Rose.'

He drew in a deep breath and ran his fingers up through his thick brown hair. The intimacy of the moment was gone; now it was back to business. 'Yes?'

'Well, don't think I'm trying to tell you how to run things, but . . . you *do* advertise the hotel, don't you?'

'Of course. Anywhere and everywhere.'

'But who do you aim your advertising at? What age-group, I mean?'

He considered, then said, 'Well, the agency I pay to promote us aims its campaigns at twenty to forty-year-olds. That's what they call the 'target audience' for winter sports. Why?'

Nicci had thought all this out last night, before going to bed. Andrew's plight had played on her mind, and she had been determined to try to find a way of helping him.

Now, however, actually putting those thoughts into words made her feel slightly nervous. 'It's just that I . . . I think you're trying to appeal to the wrong market.'

'Eh?'

Before she could explain, he held up one palm. 'Hang on,' he said. 'I don't know about you, but I'm starving. Let's discuss this over breakfast.'

Twenty minutes later, *Frau* Blucher, a large, good-natured fifty-year-old whose dark hair was pulled back in an unflattering bun, brought them a typical offering of coffee, bread rolls, cheese and jam, which the Swiss called the *café complet*.

'Now,' Andrew said, 'what were you saying about me aiming at the wrong market?'

The extra time had given Nicci a better chance to organise her thoughts, and now she spoke with surprising clarity.

'Well, don't misunderstand what I'm going to say,' she began. 'The Rose is a wonderful old building. It's got character and elegance and style. But as you yourself have admitted, it can't hope to compete with a modern hotel such as the Anderberg, where all the facilities have been designed specifically for young people who want an active holiday.'

'That's true enough,' he admitted.

'Then why do you still target that

younger end of the market, when you know you can't give them what they want?'

He frowned. 'Why, because . . . because, as I say, that's the main audience for winter sports' holidays.'

'I may be wrong,' she said, 'but I think you should try to attract families and older holiday-makers. For one thing, I think older people, retired couples, would have a greater appreciation of these marvellous surroundings. I doubt whether they, or parents with young children, would necessarily be interested in saunas or solariums or skiing, but they *might* enjoy all the nature trails you have nearby.'

She felt disappointed when he made no immediate comment. He chewed on a piece of bread for a moment, then looked at her. 'Go on,' he said.

She perked up a bit. 'Well, there really isn't much more to say. As far as I can see, everyone caters for this so-called 'target audience', but nobody bothers with the young families and older couples, and I'm certain there's a great many of them who would love to visit towns like Anderberg, and enjoy all the comforts of home that the Rose could offer.'

Nicci finished speaking and waited patiently for a reaction, but Andrew didn't say a word. He reached for his coffee cup and drank slowly. Nicci watched him closely, feeling foolish. At last, miserably, she said, 'If it's a bad idea, just say so.'

'Well,' he sighed, 'it *is* a bit obvious, really, isn't it? So obvious, in fact — that I'd never given it a thought!'

'What?'

His face broke into a smile and his eyes took on a bright, inspired glow. 'It's brilliant!' he said, reaching out to squeeze her hand affectionately. 'You're absolutely right, of course! There *is* nowhere for the people you mention! I can't think why it's never occurred to me before!'

She could see that his mind was already racing ahead, fired by her suggestion. 'You think there's merit in it, then?' she asked.

He switched his gaze back to her and squeezed her hand again, sending an electric tingle up her arm. 'Nicci — I think it's got so *much* merit that I'm going to fix up another meeting with my bank manager to see what *he* thinks of it!'

★ ★ ★

Later that day, Nicci and Karen decided to go on a sight-seeing trip to the nearby town of Engelstock. According to the guidebook, it was a quaint but picturesque little hamlet with magnificent gardens and regular boating trips across a lake two miles wide.

Catching one of the bright yellow buses on the northern edge of town, they spent the thirty-minute ride swapping news. Not surprisingly, Karen's main topic of conversation was Leno. It appeared that they were growing more and more enamoured of each other, and Nicci was pleased that her friend should be having such an exciting time.

She was feeling much happier in herself, too. It pleased her more than she could say to have had Andrew react the way he had to her suggestion. When they had met that evening in town, he had just about given up his struggle to keep the family business going. The last time she saw him, just before coming out to meet Karen, she had seen a new sense of purpose within him, and it filled her with joy.

Engelstock turned out to be everything the guide books had said it would. Surrounded by lush meadows and the odd, orderly stand of fruit trees, the hamlet resembled something out of a fairy tale, and the girls had a wonderful day seeing the sights and sampling the charming Swiss hospitality of the townsfolk.

Again Nicci noticed that the weather was crisp, cool and dry, though. The blue sky above gave not even the vaguest promise of snow.

6

That evening, Andrew came into the dining-room and hurried over to Nicci's table. They hadn't seen each other since Nicci had returned from Engelstock, and now her heart leapt at the sight of him.

'Please, don't let me disturb you,' he said, indicating the shredded and fried potatoes on the plate in front of her. '*Frau* Blucher's *Rosti* should never be interrupted, but I won't keep you a minute.'

'Don't worry about it,' said Nicci. 'Stay for as long as you like.'

Andrew sat down opposite her. 'I just wanted to tell you, I rang my bank manager this afternoon. At first he thought I was just trying to get another extension on my overdraft, but when I told him about your idea, he sat up and took notice.'

Nicci finished chewing a piece of potato. 'Does that mean he'll grant you a reprieve?' she asked eagerly.

'Not necessarily,' Andrew replied. 'But he must think I'm on to something, otherwise he wouldn't have agreed to let me see him to discuss it further.'

Her smile was loving. 'I'm so pleased for you.'

'Well, don't be — not yet, anyway. We've a lot of water to cross yet before we're home and dry.'

'We?'

He looked faintly embarrassed. 'Well, I was just wondering . . . Have you got anything planned for tomorrow? It's just that I've got to be in Zurich to see my bank manager at ten o'clock, and I thought perhaps you might care to have lunch with me afterwards.'

Nicci was surprised by the invitation, but pleasantly so. She and Karen had made no firm plans for the day, and she could always tell her friend about her trip into the city when she saw her tonight at the ice rink.

'This is all down to you, after all,' Andrew said sincerely. 'Without you, I'd still be planning to close up at the end of April. At least now I'm in with another chance to try and keep the old place going.'

Her smile widened. 'All right, thank you very much.'

Andrew appeared relieved. 'I was hoping you'd say that,' he said. 'It's ridiculous, I know, but I think I've come to look upon you as my lucky charm.'

She was flattered. 'Oh?'

He nodded. 'Yes. Ever since I met you my luck's just been getting better and better.'

★   ★   ★

After breakfasting together the next morning, Nicci returned to her room to get her jacket while Andrew quickly imparted some last-minute instructions to *Frau* Blucher.

As Nicci came back downstairs, the grey-eyed hotelier was saying, 'Now, you're *sure* you'll be all right on your own?'

Frau Blucher, installed behind the reception desk, bobbed her head and smiled. '*Ja, ja*, off course. There iss not so much work here at the Rose that an old professional like me can't cope,' she said.

He returned her smile. 'Well, make the most of the lull, *Frau* Blucher. If everything goes according to plan today, we'll be drawing in more business than we know what to do with!'

The Swiss woman reached out to touch him on the arm. 'I hope so, Andrew. But don't be too disappointed if it goes the other way.'

Andrew turned to face Nicci. She wore a cream-coloured blouse and tailored navy blue trousers, and a neat red bow was tied at her neck. The outfit was at once both smart and casual, and would fit in with whichever type of restaurant Andrew decided to take her to.

'Ready?' he asked expectantly.

She nodded.

Outside, Nicci automatically prepared to set off for the bus stop at the corner of the street, but Andrew stopped her and pointed in the opposite direction. '*This* way,' he said.

'But I thought — '

' — that we had to get to Anderberg Station?' He shook his head. 'No. Today's a special occasion. Win or lose, we're making *this* journey in style.'

He led her down a side-street that brought them out to the rear of the hotel, and opened the passenger door of a parked Mercedes.

Nicci stared at the vehicle. She didn't know much about vintage cars, but this model was so immaculate that she knew instinctively that it was probably a highly-prized collector's item.

'Style isn't the word for it,' she remarked, climbing inside.

'Yes, it's a lovely old car, isn't it?' he

agreed. 'It was my father's. I don't use it much, but today I thought I'd make an exception.'

He closed the door behind her and hurried around to slip behind the steering wheel. The interior of the Mercedes was spotless, and hinted at good, old-fashioned quality in much the same way as the hotel.

He started the engine and they slowly pulled away from the Rose. Within a few minutes they were cruising smoothly along Anderberg's quiet streets.

'I hope you didn't have to cancel anything special with your friend Karen,' he said as they left the town behind them and began to follow the winding country road north.

'No. She said she'd probably spend the day on the slopes.'

'With her skiing instructor?'

'Yes. They seem to get on well together.'

When he said no more, Nicci glanced at his profile. 'Are you nervous?' she asked quietly.

He smiled. 'Terrified. But I have such faith in your idea that I can't help but feel wildly confident, too. You know, the Rose has always been a family hotel. I don't know why I ever tried to make it appeal to a different market.'

'You only did what you thought best,' she pointed out.

'True. But look where it's got me.'

'It's not too late, though, Andrew. If you can only convince your bank manager that you can make this new idea work . . . '

'*Herr* Kessler is a hard man to convince about *anything*,' Andrew said. 'But you can be sure I'm going to be as persuasive as I can.'

As the kilometres unwound, Nicci asked her companion about Frau Blucher. 'She seems very fond of you.'

'She should be,' he said with a laugh. 'She's known me from the minute I was born. Quite literally, in fact.'

'She helped to deliver you?'

'There was no 'help' about it; she *did* deliver me, all by herself,' he replied.

'She's worked at the Rose for more than thirty years, ever since my parents first opened the place, in fact. She's been a good and loyal employee, and a wonderful friend. Without her, I think we'd have gone under long before now.' He took a corner and sent them along another straight, practically empty country road. 'Sometimes I think *Frau* Blucher knows more about running the Rose than I do. It became a very important part of her life after her husband died a few years ago.'

'She's certainly a very nice woman.'

'You know, it's crazy, but . . . all these years of struggling to keep the old place going . . . I only really did it for the sake of my parents and *Frau* Blucher. What *I* wanted never seemed to enter into it, somehow.'

'And now?'

'Now, thanks to you,' he said, 'I realise that this *is* what I want; to continue the tradition, leave something behind for my children, if I'm ever lucky enough to find a woman who'll have me. It's what I think I've wanted all along, but I just didn't know it.'

Nicci stared out at the flower-dotted meadows blurring past the passenger-side window in a riot of colour. She thought about fate, and how it had brought them together. She felt that just knowing this kind and sensitive man had somehow enriched her, and hopefully she had brought something to *his* life, too.

As they drew ever nearer to Zurich, she remembered how the Rose Hotel had drawn her to it right from the very first. She hadn't even known what it was then, it had just been a square building with red bricks and powder blue paint.

In a peculiar way she felt she should be grateful to Peter Clark for having made her move out of the Anderberg and go to stay in the Rose's opulent environs, to get to know Andrew Thornton better, and to share this one last chance of keeping his family business going.

Once again she glanced at Andrew's

profile. 'Good luck with *Herr* Kessler,' she said. 'I'll be thinking of you.'

He smiled up at her reflection in the rear-view mirror. 'My lucky charm,' he said.

They reached the city half an hour before Andrew's appointment, found a place to park the car and walked through the bustling streets feeling a little nervous together.

Finally they came to a halt before a very modern building, all chrome and smoked-glass windows, that looked like no bank Nicci had ever seen before. Just the sight of the imposing structure was enough to give her butterflies.

'Well, how do I look?' Andrew asked, turning to face her.

He was wearing a black suit, white shirt and sky-blue tie. In his right hand he held a briefcase which contained all the notes he'd typed up the night before, and which he would use today as the basis for his discussions. Nicci inspected him and felt tremendously proud.

'Like a winner,' she said with an

encouraging smile.

He nodded. 'Thanks.'

On impulse she reached up and pecked him on the cheek. The warmth of his skin was intoxicating.

He was surprised by the gesture, but appreciative. He checked his watch and sighed. 'With any luck, I should only be a couple of hours. Shall I meet you back here at, say, twelve?'

'I'll be waiting,' she said.

Andrew straightened his tie one last time and then went into the bank.

With so much time to kill, Nicci decided to do some more sight-seeing, but despite everything that Zurich had to offer, she couldn't get Andrew out of her mind.

Although she kept telling herself that it was impossible for her to have fallen in love with a man she'd only known for such a short space of time, the knowledge that she would never see him again after she and Karen returned home to England left her feeling hollow and dejected.

Indeed, thinking of home reminded her of the electrical components firm and her deadening job in the accounts department. At last she saw everything in perspective. She had no doubt that she would live down the embarrassment Peter had caused her. Oh, she had been the subject of some gossip, yes, but that gossip wouldn't last forever, and soon another topic would come along to occupy the minds of her colleagues.

But did she really want to continue working where she was? This holiday had opened up a whole new horizon for her. Helping Andrew take his fight to keep the Rose Hotel in business one stage further had made her feel restless, anxious to find a challenge of her own.

Strolling along Zurich's busy streets, Nicci peered through the windows of private art galleries and wandered up and down the narrow, hilly avenues of the Old Town. She spent a long time admiring the fine old mansions that lined the shores of the River Limmat.

But her thoughts remained troubled all the while.

At last it was time to head back to the bank and her rendezvous with Andrew. Again she hoped that he'd been successful in his quest. She knew how shattered he would be if he wasn't.

She took the fact that he was already waiting for her as a bad sign. That his meeting with *Herr* Kessler hadn't taken as long as he'd thought implied that they'd either run out of things to discuss — or that *Herr* Kessler was of the opinion that there was nothing worth discussing in the first place.

As she hurried up to him he reached out and took her hand in a gesture that was completely natural. She looked eagerly up into his face, searching for some sign that might tell her what had happened, but his long, rugged countenance was unreadable.

'Have you been waiting long?' she asked.

'About twenty minutes.'

'I'm sorry. If I'd known — '

'How could you?' he asked. 'I thought I'd be in there for a couple of hours, at least.'

She sighed. 'It didn't go very well, then?'

He looked down at her. 'I'll tell you over lunch,' he replied soberly.

★   ★   ★

'In fact,' he announced after they'd been shown to a table and he had ordered for them in German, 'it went okay.'

She watched his face carefully. 'But no more than that?'

Andrew glanced around the restaurant, which was softly-lit and well-patronised. '*Herr* Kessler was actually quite enthusiastic. He agrees that, by and large, parents with young families and older people get a raw deal from some of our resorts, and he feels that, if the Rose were to go back to catering for that market, we might be able to get back on to a firm financial footing.'

She read his tone correctly. ' 'But'?' she prompted.

'But,' he replied, '*Herr* Kessler is nothing if not a businessman, and he has his board of directors to answer to. He can't keep extending credit to such an ailing business unless that business can prove that it's still in with a fighting chance.'

Now Nicci was perplexed. 'But how can you do that?'

'By showing a profit at the end of the season.'

Nicci suddenly remembered one of their earlier conversations. 'Those two school parties from England you told me about,' she said. 'They would put you into profit, wouldn't they? Modestly so, I mean.'

'Yes,' he said sourly. 'But if you remember, they're coming over for the skiing — and unless we have some snow in the next couple of weeks, they may well decide to cancel their bookings and go elsewhere.'

Taking a sip of water, she saw the

irony of the situation. Andrew's fate hinged solely on the vagaries of the weather, and if Leno de Masi was to be believed, there would be no snow for the rest of the season!

'Still,' he said with admirable fortitude, 'we'll cross that bridge when we come to it, and in the meantime, I'll use the next month or so to put together a stronger case that Kessler can present to his board.'

'Maybe I can help you.'

He smiled. 'You've done more than enough already. Besides, you're supposed to be on holiday. *Enjoying* yourself.'

'I *am* enjoying myself.'

After the meal, they went for a walk around the city together. It was still fairly early, and there was little need to rush back, for as Andrew had told her a couple of days before, the Rose practically ran itself when bookings were so low.

They visited the Reitberg Museum, window-shopped in the city's underground shopping mall, then stopped for coffee at one of the many cafés lining the Bahnhofstrasse. At last, as the afternoon wore on and the blue of the sky began to grow very slightly deeper, Andrew led Nicci halfway across the Quai Bridge, where they stood looking out over the Zurichsee, watching the gentle, chilly breeze ruffle its mirrorlike surface.

'I really appreciate all the help and support you've given me, Nicci,' he said sincerely. 'You'd be surprised how rare it is to find that kind of generosity.'

Nicci gave a modest shrug. 'I wouldn't go quite *that* far.'

'*I* would.'

He turned to face her and she looked up to find him frowning. In the slowly fading sunlight she saw his jaw muscles working. He looked grim, troubled, as if he were debating something, and was uncertain how best to proceed.

At last he reached out to place his palms gently on her shoulders. He pulled her towards him and she went willingly, her thoughts in a whirl and not her own.

She raised her face as Andrew brought his lips down on hers, and their kiss began gently, thoughtfully, a tender meeting of lips that grew rapidly in passion.

Nicci put her arms around him and felt wonderful in his strong but loving embrace.

At last, after some indeterminate length of time, they broke apart, each of them reluctant to end the moment. She looked up into his smoky grey eyes, and found a hint of joy where once there had only been worry and despair.

Joy made her own heart pound, too, a joy she had never known with Peter Clark. But mixed in with her feeling of euphoria was a sense of trepidation. She must not allow herself to fall in love with this man. There was no future in their relationship, not with Andrew here and Nicci in England.

Besides . . .

Besides, she had just suffered the

trauma of one broken heart, and she had no desire to suffer another. She still felt vulnerable, cynical . . . Could she bring herself to trust another man completely so soon after Peter? *Dare* she?

He bent his head to kiss her again, but this time, as much as she longed for the touch of his lips, her confidence deserted her and before she could stop herself, she was pushing him away.

He didn't fight her. He stood back, long face unreadable once more. At last he said, 'I'm sorry, I thought — '

She avoided his eyes. 'No, Andrew, it's . . . it's me.'

He returned his attention to the wind-rippled Zurichsee, doubtless to save her from further embarrassment. She stood beside him with eyes downcast, thoughts confused, feeling wretched.

A moment or so later Andrew said, 'Come on, then. We'd best be getting back.' His voice was flat, not angry, just somehow defeated.

'Andrew, I — '

'It's all right, Nicci. There's no need for explanations.' He checked his wristwatch, more for something to do than to actually find out the time. 'Come on.'

They made their way back to the car in an awkward, uncomfortable silence. Nicci was more annoyed with herself than she could say. If only she had the confidence to fall in love again! But there was always the memory of Peter lurking at the back of her mind, the memory of how he had taken her trust and abused it.

Were all men the same, though, she wondered? Of course not. And Nicci was certain that Andrew would never let her down. And yet . . .

No. Her love . . . *their* love . . . was impossible, without a future. He belonged here, with the Rose. And she . . . ?

Miserably she wondered if she really belonged *anywhere*.

On the journey back to Anderberg, Andrew made a brave attempt at conversation. He spoke of the ideas he'd had to attract an older clientele back to the hotel, and the facilities he hoped to introduce for parents with young children. He was imaginative and earnest, but Nicci's thoughts were too troubled to allow her to relax and add her own suggestions.

The sunset was breathtaking. It bathed the sky with a wide streak of amber. Scudding clouds followed them south, building into dark, billowing giants as they approached their destination.

'Would you like me to drop you off at the Anderberg Hotel?' he asked after a particularly long silence. 'I didn't know if you might want to see your friend.'

Her heart went out to him. Despite the fact that she had rejected him, he was still considerate of her wishes, the perfect gentleman.

'No thank you,' she replied stiffly. 'I think I'll go straight up to my room, take a bath and have an early night.'

He nodded without taking his eyes

off the road. 'I understand. It's been a long day.'

Although they didn't know it, however, the day was just about to grow longer. Pulling the Mercedes into the courtyard behind the Rose, Andrew switched off the engine and turned to face her.

Nicci was already reaching for the door handle, anxious to avoid any further distress, but feeling his eyes on her she froze. As wrapped up in her own emotions as she surely was, she could not ignore him. If he had something to say, then the least she could do was listen. He deserved that small courtesy, and much, much more, and she extended it now.

'Nicci,' he said softly, his face shadowed in the lowering light. 'I'm sorry, for this afternoon, I mean. I didn't intend to force myself onto you — '

'You didn't.'

'But I upset you, that much was obvious.' He swallowed. 'Well, I just wanted you to know that I was sorry, and that . . . that it won't happen again.'

She should have been relieved that it was all over before it had really started. She should have thanked her lucky stars for having avoided yet more heartache. But curiously, his promise to leave her alone from this point forward made something inside her wither and die, and she fought against a swell of emotion that almost choked her.

They climbed out of the car and walked around to the front of the Rose. By now it was nearing five o'clock, and the sun was a bright orange sliver just visible behind the ragged mountains to the west. The entire vista was one of seemingly perfect peace.

As soon as they entered the reception, however, Andrew and Nicci both realised that something was far from peaceful in their immediate vicinity. Over at the desk, *Frau* Blucher was doing her best to calm the distressed parents of young David and Jennifer Blake.

Andrew took charge at once. Striding forward, he demanded to know what was wrong.

The children's father turned to face him, looking worried and desperate. 'They've vanished!' he said urgently. 'David and Jenny . . . we can't find them anywhere!'

Nicci deliberately stayed in the background, unwilling to add to the parents' distress by crowding them. But she knew a sudden stab of alarm at the news, and her thoughts automatically went out to the parents.

'What exactly do you mean?' Andrew asked, his clear, compelling tone cutting through the parents' worry and confusion.

'Well,' said their mother, dabbing at eyes sore from crying, 'we . . . we all sp-spent the day out at the . . . the ice rink . . . and then we came b-back here . . . about half an hour ago . . . '

'David was showing off,' the children's

father interrupted, obviously at his wits'
end. 'He wanted to stay at the ice rink,
you see, and didn't want to come away.
Anyway, we got back here, went up to
our room, and then suddenly Louise
here noticed that the kids had gone
missing!'

'You've searched the hotel?' Andrew
asked *Frau* Blucher.

'But off course. It was the first thing I
did.'

'And you didn't see the children go
past the desk here, out into the street?'

'No. But I was not here all the time. I
spent perhaps ten or fifteen minutes in
the kitchen, preparing the evening meal.'

Andrew allowed the facts to sink
in. Nicci watched his weathered face
closely. He looked even more grim now
than he had back at the Quai Bridge,
if that were possible. His mind was
racing. His concern was obvious. At
last he reached a decision.

'All right. Let's assume that the
children *did* go out. Is there anywhere
else they might have gone, Mr Blake?

Apart from the ice rink, I mean. A favourite place?'

The worried father tried to bring order to his preoccupied mind and shook his head. 'No . . . nowhere that I can think of . . . '

Nicci suddenly stepped forward. 'What about the nature trails on the slopes behind the hotel?' she asked. All eyes turned to her. 'I mean . . . David *did* tell me the other day that he wanted to be a mountaineer when he grew up. Perhaps — '

'Yes!' said Mrs Blake. 'Yes, he's forever going on about climbing hills!'

'All right,' Andrew said authoritatively. 'My advice to you, Mr Blake, is to go back to the ice rink and see if the children have returned there. I'll check the slopes out back. *Frau* Blucher, telephone the local constabulary, if you would be so kind. Give them the children's description and ask them to keep a look-out.'

Suddenly the reception became a hive of activity as the small group set about finding the missing children. Andrew set his briefcase down on the desk and turned back to the double doors through which they'd just come. As he did so, he saw Nicci watching him through moist eyes, and quickly averted his gaze.

'Andrew — '

He looked at her this time. 'Yes?'

'I'm going with you.'

He shook his head. 'You don't know these slopes. You'd only slow me down.'

Her lips firmed down in determination. 'I've *got* to lend a hand.'

His sigh was heavy. 'All right, then, come on. There's a flashlight in the car. We'll use that.'

They hurried out into the twilight together.

★ ★ ★

The night was turning cold. Stars twinkled distantly overhead. Andrew and Nicci hurried back to the yard behind the hotel, retrieved Andrew's flashlight from the glove compartment of the Mercedes and quickly closed the distance between the rear of the hotel and the thickly-forested slopes rising majestically towards the dusky sky.

'You *do* realise just how far these nature trails stretch, I suppose?' he said as they began their ascent. Within moments the pines to either side had swallowed them up. 'I didn't want to dash Mrs Blake's hopes, so I didn't say anything just now, but they wind for tens of kilometres in all directions.'

'But how far could two small children go in just over half an hour?' she argued.

'You'd be surprised.'

He switched on the flashlight and began sweeping the corn-yellow beam back and forth, chasing away shadows here, creating new ones there.

'*David!*' he called. '*Jennifer!*'

Nicci began to call out the children's names too, but there came no answer. Andrew climbed higher and Nicci hurried after him. Behind them, Anderberg sprawled across the valley floor, toy-size

161

from this distance and elevation, with little lights glowing and twinkling at windows and doors.

'*David!* Can you hear me? It's Nicci, from the hotel!'

'Perhaps they're hiding,' Andrew said, probing the darkness for any signs of movement. 'You know, maybe they realise they've done something bad, and they're scared of the consequences.'

Nicci nodded her agreement, for the same thing had occurred to her.

Together they hiked deeper into the forest, their footsteps muted by a carpet of fallen pine needles. The beam of the flashlight swept one way, then the other. Nocturnal birds called and sang, disturbed by the two searching humans, but there was no sound or movement other than that.

Twenty minutes later Nicci shook her head in despair. 'It's like trying to find a needle in a haystack,' she said tiredly.

He nodded, pausing to take a breather. '*David! Jennifer!*'

There was no response.

'Well, don't get too despondent,' he said consolingly. 'Maybe they're not up here for the finding. Given the circumstances, I should think it far more likely that they went back to the ice rink.'

'Maybe.'

He frowned across at her moon-splashed profile. 'You don't sound too convinced.'

She shrugged. 'I can't help it. I just have this . . . I don't know, *instinct*, I suppose you'd call it.'

'Female intuition?'

'Something like that.'

'You feel certain they came this way, then?'

'I don't know why, but . . . yes.'

'Come on, then. Let's put your instincts to the test.'

'But what if I'm wrong?' she asked worriedly. 'I could be sending us on a wild-goose chase, Andrew.'

He smiled a smile of encouragement at her. 'Your instincts haven't been wrong since I've known you,' he replied. 'Come on — *I've* got faith in you, even if you haven't.'

7

They followed the nature trails higher, trending north, then south in winding, 'S'-shaped patterns in order to search a wider area in less time. The forest swallowed up their voices as they called to the missing children. But at no time did they see or hear anything to make them believe they were on the right track.

'Oh, this is hopeless!' Nicci said when another fifteen minutes of wasted effort lay behind them. 'I was wrong, Andrew. I *must* have been. No children as young as David and Jennifer could have come this far in such a short space of time.'

Secretly Andrew had to agree. Perhaps at the lower elevations there had been a possibility, albeit remote, that they might locate the little ones. But this far up, it began to look increasingly unlikely that they would find them.

He studied Nicci's sad face carefully in the gentle glow cast by the flashlight and saw frustration and disappointment plain on her beautiful countenance. He waited a moment before asking, 'Do you want to carry on, or turn back, then?'

She shrugged helplessly, peering into the darkness around them, through branches and past sturdy tree-trunks. At last, in a small, defeated tone, she said, 'Turn back, I suppose.'

Although he had promised not to make any further advances towards her, Andrew reached out now to put a comforting arm around her shoulders and squeeze her gently. 'Hey, don't take it so hard. It doesn't really matter that you were wrong, does it? So long as the children turn up safe and sound?'

She looked up at him. Though he was trying to cheer her up, she could tell by the look in his eyes that he was still gravely concerned for David and Jennifer.

'Come on, then,' she sighed. 'Perhaps we'll have good news waiting for us when we get back to the Rose.'

'Let's hope so.'

Together they began to trudge dejectedly back down the wooded slopes, in silence and with the flashlight pointing the way ahead. They went perhaps twenty feet, certainly no more, and then Andrew came to an abrupt halt.

'No,' he said.

She looked up at him enquiringly. 'Andrew?'

'No,' he repeated, more firmly this time. 'Come on, Nicci — we're going to keep looking.'

'But — '

His expression was earnest as he looked down at her. 'Do your instincts still tell you the children came this way?' he asked.

Nicci didn't know what to think anymore. In her mind she saw little David Blake telling her that he wanted to be a mountaineer when he grew up.

She remembered Mrs Blake saying that David was forever going on about climbing hills.

She said, 'I don't know, Andrew. I — '

'Yes or no?'

Forced to decide, she said, 'Yes.'

Although his face was difficult to see in the poor light, there was no mistaking the determination in his tone. 'Come on, then.'

'But . . . but why? I thought — '

'It's like I said just now. Your instincts haven't been wrong since I've known you. Why should they fail you now?' Taking her by one arm, he began to climb higher once more. 'Remember the day we collided on the slopes behind the Anderberg Hotel?' he asked. 'We didn't really know each other at all then, and yet you knew *instinctively* that I had something on my mind. And what about yesterday morning, over breakfast? You don't know anything about the hotel trade, and yet you know *instinctively* that I was trying to cater

167

for the wrong type of clientele!'

They were moving faster up the slope now, and Andrew was sweeping the torch-beam back and forth before them in slow, searching arcs. '*David*! *Jennifer*! It's all right, nobody's going to hurt you! Come on, we just want to take you back to the hotel!'

'David! Jennifer!'

Nicci's heart began to race. Andrew was right. Why *should* her instincts fail her now? She was sure the children were up here somewhere. The only question was — where?

Suddenly they both stopped in the middle of the trail, listening. From just beyond the torchlight they heard another sound. A tingle washed across Nicci's face. She exchanged a look with Andrew.

'David!' she called tremulously. 'Jennifer? Is that you?'

There was no reply, but Nicci thought she saw a movement ahead and to her right. 'Andrew, quickly — shine the beam over there.'

He did as she asked, then drew in a sharp breath as two pale faces were suddenly illuminated in the circle of light.

Nicci's bottom lip quivered. 'Children! It's all right! It's me, Nicci!'

And David and Jennifer Blake hurried down the trail towards her, faces screwed up, tears streaming down their smudged cheeks, each of them sobbing, 'I want my mummy! I want my mummy!'

★　★　★

'It all sounds very exciting,' Karen pronounced after Nicci finished recounting the story over lunch at a mid-town café the following lunchtime. 'A real adventure. Too bad I missed it.'

Now that Nicci had finished speaking, she began toying with the food on her plate. But she had no real appetite today, and was feeling somewhat detached from events around her thanks largely to a near-sleepless night.

'The kids were reunited with their

parents all right, I take it?' Karen prompted.

Nicci nodded. 'Oh yes. It was all very tearful, but at the same time it was a wonderful moment.'

'I'll bet.'

Nicci lost herself again for one brief moment as she recalled the scene they'd just been discussing. There hadn't been a dry eye in the reception once the children were reunited with their frantic parents. Mr and Mrs Blake had been eager to express their gratitude. *Frau* Blucher had retired hurriedly to the kitchen, to blow her nose and wipe her eyes. And looking up suddenly, Nicci had discovered Andrew watching her with such fierce pride that she had coloured immediately.

Once again she had felt a confused blend of emotions. On the one hand she wanted to melt into Andrew's arms, to love him and be loved by him forever. But there was a barrier between them, a barrier of fear and uncertainty; fear that he might one day abuse her trust and break her heart as Peter had done, uncertainty over how their relationship could ever flourish with Andrew here and she back in England . . .

With a few muttered words, she had excused herself and hurried up to her room, there to lock herself away and try in vain to sort out the chaotic mixture of emotions that continued to bedevil her even today.

'Are you feeling all right, Nic?' Karen asked with a frown. 'You've hardly touched your meal.'

'What? Oh, sure. I'm just not all that hungry.'

But Karen knew her too well to be fobbed off with a quick white lie. 'Are you sure?' she asked sceptically. 'I know you've been busy, whizzing off to Zurich and traipsing half-way up those mountains behind the Rose, but you seem . . . I don't know, preoccupied somehow. Down in the dumps.'

Nicci forced a smile to allay her friend's suspicions. 'You're imagining it,' she said, pushing her uneaten lunch aside. 'Anyway, how goes it with your Latin Lothario?'

'Eh?'

'Leno.'

'Oh, fine.' Karen shrugged and took a sip of coffee. 'He's still absolutely besotted with me, so he obviously has good taste.'

'Oh, obviously.'

'He wanted to take me to the Oberalp Pass this afternoon, but I told him that enough was enough. I came on this holiday to spend time with you . . . though I must say, I've seen you looking happier.'

Nicci pretended not to hear the question in her friend's voice. Still, she had reached an important decision after her more-or-less sleepless night, and she would have to tell Karen about it sooner or later.

Karen pre-empted that moment by saying, 'Come on, Nic — out with it. Remember what they say; 'A problem shared makes two people miserable'.'

Nicci smiled fondly at the girl across

the table from her. 'Oh well, you might as well hear it sooner or later. It's . . . it's about Andrew.'

Karen was at once on the defensive. 'Attila the Hun? What's he done this time?'

'Nothing. He's been thoughtful, kind, generous . . . the perfect gentleman.'

Karen studied her friend very carefully. After a weighty pause she said, 'Are you by any chance telling me that you've fallen in love with him?'

Not trusting herself to speak, Nicci only nodded.

'How does he feel about you? Do you know?'

It was Nicci's turn to shrug. 'I can't say for sure, of course, but . . . but I think the feeling's mutual.'

'So what's the problem?'

'*Me*,' Nicci said despairingly, being careful to keep her voice down. 'I know it's silly, but I just can't help it . . . After Peter, I just find it so hard to *trust* another man, no matter how much I know for a *fact* that he'll never let me down. I just feel so *wary* all the time, so . . . so vulnerable. I'm absolutely terrified of getting hurt again.'

Karen finished her coffee, her expression now as troubled as that of her friend. 'Sooner or later,' she pronounced at length, 'you're going to have to trust *someone*. I mean, you can't tar every man with the same brush for the rest of your life.'

'I know that. But I just think that all this . . . what I feel for Andrew, and what I think he feels for me . . . it's all happened so quickly. What do I really know about him? He's behaved faultlessly so far, but is that reason enough for me to trust him?'

'Only you can answer that,' Karen replied gently. 'And the only advice I can offer you is to follow those instincts you were just telling me about.'

'But what if my instincts are wrong? What then?'

Karen shook her head. 'I don't know, love. I really don't know.'

Nicci cleared her throat. 'Anyway,'

she said reluctantly, 'I've already reached a decision, and I only hope you won't think I've let you down by taking it.'

Karen's frown asked the question.

'I'm leaving Anderberg,' Nicci announced miserably.

Karen's reaction was predictable. 'Oh, come *on*, now! You can't keep running away, Nic! Look, you left the Anderberg Hotel because of Peter. Now you're leaving the Rose because of Andrew! Where will you go next? You'll never find a room at one of the guest houses, they're all full!'

'That doesn't matter, Kar. Didn't you hear what I just said? I'm *leaving* Anderberg.' Tears filled her hazel eyes and she quickly blinked them away. 'I'm going back to England,' she said, stifling a sob.

Karen was dumbstruck. 'Going — ? When?'

Nicci's voice dropped to a whisper. 'This afternoon.'

★   ★   ★

Karen made a valiant effort to talk her out of it, of course. Nicci had expected as much. But her mind was made up. She was confused; about herself, about Andrew, about what she really wanted for her future; and she needed time and distance to sort herself out.

So she was running away.

Naturally, she felt bad about letting Karen down. It wasn't going to be much of a holiday for her, left here alone. Still, at least she had Leno, and that would count for something.

At least that was what Nicci kept telling herself as she returned to the Rose and went straight up to her room, to pack her things away and prepare for the long trek back to Zurich. She knew she must justify her actions to herself, or lose her nerve completely.

She had spent the morning phoning around to confirm the availability of a flight back to England. There was one leaving Kloten Airport at five o'clock this afternoon.

Nicci intended to be on it.

Provided everything went according to plan, she should be touching down at Heathrow sometime after six-thirty. She could be home just after seven, back in familiar surroundings, consoled by an understanding mother and sister, and all of this would seem just like a dream, as if it had never really happened.

She finished packing and stowed her gear behind the door. Then she sat at the dressing-table and took a sheet of hotel stationery from the neat stack in front of her.

With a heavy heart, she began to write Andrew a note, but it took a long while to phrase it correctly, to tell him exactly what she was doing, and why. As she wrote, she remembered those first few hours in Switzerland, Karen waving to the two young Zurchers, their first encounter with Andrew, the pictur-esque train ride here to Anderberg.

She wanted very badly to cry.

It was only a sudden light rapping at the door that made her hold back the tears. Drawing in a deep breath and struggling to compose herself, she turned around on the neat little chair — lavender, like the walls of this, the Rose Room — and said, 'Yes?'

The door opened and Andrew lingered in the doorway. 'I hope I'm not interrupting . . . ?'

She fought to disguise the tremor in her voice, to sound normal, casual. 'No, no. Come in, Andrew. What can I do for you?'

Andrew came in and closed the door. Because she had been hoping to leave without his knowing, she felt a sudden jolt of fear that he would notice her luggage. But fortunately — for her — he was too preoccupied.

Clearing his throat self-consciously, he said, 'I just wondered if you were all right. I haven't seen you since last night.'

'Oh, I'm fine. I've been out most of the morning, and I had lunch with Karen.' She had deliberately chosen to stay out of his way, before further contact with him weakened her resolve and exposed her to the possibility of more heartache.

He crossed the room and glanced through one of the windows. 'It's just that . . . ever since yesterday afternoon . . . ' He struggled to find the right words, as awkward now as she had been writing her note just a few minutes earlier. 'I wouldn't want you to think you have to avoid me,' he said at last.

She made no comment.

'You've come to mean a great deal to me over the last few days,' he continued. 'Perhaps more than you should. And . . . well, I suppose I flattered myself that you felt the same way about me.'

He smiled to take some of the tension out of the air, but it didn't work. 'I never would have kissed you if I'd known it would ruin things between us,' he said sincerely.

'You've no need to apologise,' she said without looking at him.

He drew in a breath. 'But tell me

something. Call it vanity, but . . . Is it that you don't feel anything for me? Or is it that you still love that other fellow?'

She was surprised. 'Peter? No, no, I'm over Peter now. It . . . it's just me, Andrew. Just the way I am.'

'We're still friends, then? I haven't blotted my copy-book too badly?'

'You haven't blotted it at all,' she said, wishing she had the courage to tell him outright of her decision to leave.

Relief was plain on his face. 'Good, I just wanted to make sure. I've fixed up a meeting with the agency who handles all our publicity for this afternoon, you see, and I didn't want to spend the rest of the day wondering.'

'I understand. I . . . I hope it all goes well for you.'

'I'm sure it will,' he replied.

They were both very much aware that she hadn't really answered his question, but he chose not to pursue it. Instead he went back over to the door, grim, a little sad, but putting on a brave face. 'I'll see you later, perhaps, tell you how I got on?'

'Perhaps,' she replied vaguely.

He opened the door, and it suddenly occurred to her that this would be the last time she ever saw him. Before she could stop herself, she said, 'Goodbye, Andrew.'

He paused and glanced back at her. A frown puckered his brow. There was something about the way she'd said the words that sounded so final, and he was sure he hadn't just imagined it. He held her gaze for a long, heavy moment, then nodded slowly, almost as if he knew what she was planning to do, and saw the futility in trying to make her stay.

His voice was quiet and dignified.

'Goodbye, Nicci.'

He closed the door softly behind him.

Half an hour later, by which time he had left for his appointment, Nicci gathered up her things and with one last look around, left the room and hurried downstairs.

Frau Blucher was polishing the double doors. Hearing footsteps behind her, she turned with a smile on her face. The smile was quickly replaced by a look of surprise when she saw that Nicci was carrying her knapsack and case, however, though she refrained from making any comment.

Fighting her embarrassment, Nicci said, 'I . . . I'm leaving now, *Frau* Blucher. I wonder if I could settle my account?'

'Off course,' the older woman said with a stiff, Germanic nod of the head. 'Everything is in order?' she asked. 'There is nothing wrong?'

'No, nothing wrong. I . . . I've just decided to cut my stay short.'

'Does Master Andrew know?'

Nicci swallowed. 'No,' she confessed. 'It's . . . it's been a spur-of-the-moment thing. But I've written him this note. I wonder if you could give it to him later?'

The Swiss woman took the note and slipped it into the pocket of her crisp white apron. 'I will make sure he gets it at the earliest opportunity.'

'*Danke.*'

Frau Blucher consulted the register and named a figure. As Nicci paid her, the older woman said, 'You know, off course, that Master Andrew will be very sorry to have missed you.'

'Yes,' Nicci said wretchedly. 'I know.'

The Swiss woman reached out to take hold of one of her hands. 'Goodbye, my dear. Take care.'

'Goodbye, *Frau* Blucher.'

Holding back a sudden tidal wave of emotion, Nicci fled the hotel and hurried down the narrow, cobbled street to the bus-stop. Overhead the sky was leaden. Heavy clouds rushed by in a grey, billowing stampede. It seemed for all the world as if the sun, which had stopped shining in Nicci's heart, had even deserted the sky, too.

She caught the first bright yellow bus that came along and alighted outside Anderberg Station a quarter of an hour later. As they'd arranged earlier, Karen was already there, waiting to see her off.

As soon as the girls were close enough they embraced, each as tearful as the other.

'You'll be all right?' Karen asked, giving her friend a squeeze and patting her gently on the shoulder, as much to comfort herself as anything else.

'Yes,' Nicci replied with a nod. 'I'm just sorry that it's ended up like this. Are you sure you don't mind me leaving you all alone?'

Karen held her at arm's length. 'Of course not — so long as this is what you really want.'

Nicci brushed a tear from her cheek. 'I know I've let you down — '

'You *haven't* let me down, so let's not hear another word about it. Just . . . just take care of yourself, Nic, and I'll see you in a week's time.'

A cold wind sprang up as the two girls embraced one last time. Then Nicci hurried into the station, turning back just once to wave goodbye, her vision blurred by more hot, stinging tears.

A train glided into the station just over ten minutes later, and Nicci hurried aboard. From her window seat, she saw Karen still waiting near the ticket office, hands in pockets, blonde hair whipped this way and that by a strengthening wind. She raised her hand and waved once again. Karen waved back.

Then the train began to slide out of the station on its long run north to Zurich.

8

As the countryside flew past in a riot of colour and the conductor swayed back and forth along the corridor outside her compartment, Nicci lost herself in her misery. Now that she was actually on her way home, she began to question the wisdom of her decision.

She saw now that running away was not the answer to her problems, and that it never had been. Running away only made matters worse. She should meet her problems head-on, confront them like an adult and resolve them in the best, most satisfying way for all concerned.

Unfortunately, however, that realisation had come too late, and she knew that there could be no going back now. She couldn't expect people to put up with her constantly-changing mind. That was wrong, and selfish.

But knowing that only made her feel worse.

All alone in the compartment, she bowed her head in prayer, and as the miles unwound beneath her, she prayed that her leaving would not upset Andrew too badly, that his plans to keep the Rose going would work out, that Anderberg would have the snowfall he so desperately needed in order to keep the two bookings that would give him that all-important end-of-season profit *Herr* Kessler had demanded . . .

At that instant, Nicci caught a movement from the corner of her eye. Sitting forward, she peered through the window at the countryside rushing past outside. At first she saw nothing unusual. But then, suddenly, her vision of the green meadows stretching off into the mountainous distance began to grow more and more restricted as a slanting wall of snow fell heavily from the slate-grey clouds above.

Nicci's heart gave a wild leap.

Snow!

Already tearful, her eyes moistened even more as she realised what the blizzard might mean for Andrew. Salvation! Another chance for the Rose!

As she watched, the snow grew thicker. It began to cluster along the ledge outside her window, and deepen. Out on the meadows odd, misshapen patches began to form and spread as snow settled on the springy grass.

The train slowed down as visibility became even more limited. Although it was only half-past three, the snow-clouds had blotted out so much daylight that it might just as well have been midnight. But still the snow continued to fall, billions upon billions of flakes drifting to earth in a constantly shifting wall of blinding white . . .

Again the train gave a lurch as it was buffeted by the strong northerly wind, and it slowed to a crawl. All Nicci could see beyond the window now was the falling snow, drifting in ever-higher mounds along the edges of the track. The beautiful, rolling meadows of a moment ago were now buried firmly under an unbroken white mantle.

Suddenly a light appeared, flickering pale yellow through the slanting snow. Nicci saw another and another, each of them strung out at regular intervals, then a sign; ST YORAN.

They shuddered to a halt at the first station down the line, the train rocking gently from side to side as the wind shoved it this way and that. The sound of its moaning rose and fell with each new gust.

On the platform outside, there was no movement whatsoever, no passengers boarding or leaving the train. And yet the train itself continued to wait at the little station, with its creaking signs just beyond the window and its pale yellow lamps shining bravely through the gloom.

After a while a message came over the intercom system in Swiss German, but Nicci couldn't understand it. At last she heard footsteps in the corridor outside and turned expectantly as the conductor appeared, sliding her door open.

'Excuse me,' he said in careful English. 'The wind has brought down some overhead cables up ahead, *und* we must wait here until they can be repaired.'

'Oh.'

'There iss hot coffee in the waiting-room,' the conductor added, pointing through the snow-clogged window at a small pine structure just a short walk along the platform. 'It will be more comfortable to wait in there, I am thinking.'

Nicci rose and reached for her luggage. 'Yes, of course. Ah . . . do you know how long the cables will take to be repaired?'

The conductor shrugged. 'It is hard to say. In these conditions, perhaps several hours.'

'It's just that I have a flight to catch in Zurich at five o'clock.'

'I doubt you will make it,' the conductor informed her regretfully. 'I doubt any planes will be *flying* in this weather.'

Nicci nodded. 'I see. Danke.'

She zipped up her jacket and climbed down from the train. She had to fight against the wind-driven snow to reach the waiting-room, which was warm and bright. Several other passengers were already there, drinking coffee provided by the station staff, and almost as soon as Nicci found an empty corner in which to stow her gear, an elderly man in a Swiss Railways uniform offered her a steaming cup.

Nicci took the hot drink with a grateful nod. Melting snow dripped off her hair and she used a handkerchief to mop herself dry. She wondered how long it would take before she could resume her journey. If the sounds of the wind howling around the building were anything to go by, it might be quite a while.

To kill time, she decided to phone Karen. Her friend might be concerned about her, since the savage weather had descended so quickly, and she was anxious to know if the snow was settling as thickly in Anderberg as it was here.

There were four pay-phones in the waiting-room, and Nicci went over to one, looked up the number for the Anderberg Hotel and dialled. The line was poor, due, no doubt, to the weather, but eventually she got through to the hotel and asked to be put through to Miss Karen Payne in Room 404.

A moment later Karen's voice came into her ear. 'Hello?'

'Karen, it's me.'

Karen's surprise was obvious in her tone. 'Nic! You're never calling from England already!'

★   ★   ★

Andrew Thornton came stamping through the double doors of the Rose Hotel with the shoulders of his grey overcoat dusted with snow. Outside, the wind howled along the narrow cobbled street, drifting snow around the base of the building and piling it up on ledges and steps.

Although he was chilled to the bone, however, Andrew was in high spirits, and as he crossed the reception he smiled broadly at *Frau* Blucher.

'Have you seen what's happened out there?' he asked jubilantly. 'According to the weather reports I managed to pick up on the car radio, the forecasters are predicting between three and four feet of snow by the end of the night, followed by clear but cold conditions!'

The Swiss woman nodded, but said nothing.

Andrew, meanwhile, unbuttoned his overcoat and ran his fingers quickly through his windswept hair. 'This might well be the saving of us, *Frau* Blucher,' he enthused. 'I must tell Nicci the news. She's up in her room, I take it?'

At last *Frau* Blucher spoke. Quietly she said, 'She has gone, Andrew.'

He stared at the woman who had delivered him, uncomprehending. 'Gone?'

'*Ja*. Back to England.'

She watched him turn pale.

'She left a note for you,' the Swiss woman said, passing it across to him.

Swallowing hard, Andrew took the note and opened it. He had to read the contents twice before he could properly take it all in. Nicci gone? He could hardly bring himself to believe it. And yet here was the proof, and *Frau* Blucher certainly wouldn't lie about it.

Slowly he refolded the note and slipped it into his overcoat pocket. The high spirits in which he'd just entered the hotel deserted him. To *Frau* Blucher, he appeared to age before her eyes, somehow deflate.

The phone on the desk rang and the Swiss woman snatched it up quickly. '*Ja*, Rose Hotel.' She listened a moment, then said, 'Hold the line please. Andrew? It is for you.'

At first he didn't seem to hear her. Then he snapped out of his reverie and with a shuddery sigh, took the handset with a nod of thanks. 'Yes, hello?'

'Oh, Mr Thornton. It's Karen Payne

here. Nicci's friend.'

Andrew's mind was still elsewhere. Distantly he heard himself say, 'Yes. Can . . . can I help you?'

Karen said, 'No. But if we hurry, I think I can help *you*.'

'I'm sorry, I don't under — '

'Just listen, Attila. Whatever Nicci might have told you to the contrary, she'll never be happy without you. Believe me, Mr Thornton, I'm her friend. I know her better than she knows herself.' Karen paused, then said, 'She loves you, Attila. Just as much as I think you love her. But Nicci's problem is one of trust.'

Now Andrew's mind was focused and sharp. 'Maybe you'd better explain that.'

'I will. You see, it all started with a rat named Peter . . . '

★   ★   ★

Time passed slowly in the St Yoran station waiting room. Most of the passengers had been travelling with companions, and now they used the time to converse, play cards or pocket chess, or read.

In the corner, Nicci sat quietly and alone, eyes closed, thoughts flat and melancholy.

They had been stuck here now for more than two hours, and in all that time the weather had continued to batter the little station relentlessly. Still, Nicci consoled herself with the knowledge that her flight home had almost certainly been cancelled. Nothing would be moving now until the blizzard blew itself out.

So all she could do now was wait here in the bright warmth and drink endless cups of coffee to keep the winter chill at bay, and hope to find another flight back to England in the morning.

She considered calling Karen again. Earlier, though the line had been poor, it had been a marvellous tonic to hear her friend's voice. She checked her small change and sorted out enough to make another call. But then she paused, looking at the coins in her palm, remembering her encounter with Andrew in front of the underground station ticket office at Kloten Airport, when she had spilled her money all over the floor.

She remembered the way he had taken hold of her hand and sorted out the correct money for her. She recalled the pleasant tingle that contact with him had always given her.

It was ridiculous, she knew, but already she missed him terribly.

She stood up and was just about to go over to the pay-phones when the waiting-room door opened and a gust of icy, snow-dotted air blew into the room.

The train conductor closed the door behind him and smiled at the would-be travellers now facing him expectantly.

'I am pleased to tell you,' he announced as soon as he'd recovered his breath, 'that the cables haf been repaired, and that we may now continue our journey.'

A low, relieved muttering went through the other passengers, and then everyone began to gather their belongings together and file back out onto the wind-ravaged platform.

The line was surprisingly orderly as the passengers began to board the waiting train once more. All around them the snow continued to swirl and drift earthward, the wind to gust, abate, gust and die down again.

Nicci was just about to climb aboard the train when a man in front of her happened to glance away to their left and point. As she followed his hand, she saw two circles of pale white light approaching by way of the snowy roadway some distance away, growing slowly larger as the car to which the headlamps belonged ploughed a steady, determined course toward the station.

The man in front of Nicci said something in German and she shook her head. 'I'm sorry, I don't understand . . . '

The man pointed off to the approaching car once more. 'You'd have to be mad or desperate to try driving on a night like this,' he translated with a chuckle.

Nicci forced a smile. 'Oh, yes.'

She returned her curious gaze to the car just as it slewed to a halt in the station car-park thirty yards away and the driver's door flew open.

Nicci recognised the car as Andrew's vintage Mercedes just a second before her wide eyes focused on Andrew himself, racing awkwardly through the snow towards her, almost slipping as he came up the ramp at the end of the platform, righting himself, hurrying nearer.

She said his name once, soundlessly, then louder. 'Andrew?'

He was no more than thirty feet away now, his coat and hair powdered with snow, his eyelashes moist with the stuff.

'*Nicci!*'

His voice carried to the waiting passengers, deep and strong above the howling wind as Andrew half-ran, half-stumbled nearer. When he came to a halt ten feet away, his broad shoulders slumped with relief.

'Nicci, thank God I got here in time!'

'Andrew, how did you find — ' But there was no need to finish the question, because Nicci already knew the answer. 'Karen!'

He nodded, his chest rising and falling as he slowly got his breath back. 'Yes, Karen,' he replied, coming nearer. 'Karen, bless her heart.' He stood facing her, holding her with the intensity of his smoky grey gaze. 'I love you, Nicci. Can't you understand that? I'd never do anything to hurt you. I love you, and I want to go on loving you forever.'

Nicci's heart started to hammer so wildly that she almost felt giddy. 'Andrew — '

'No,' he cut in, holding up a palm for silence. 'I know all about Peter Clark, and what he did to you. Karen told me everything.' He reached up to wipe snow from his face. 'But come what may, I swear to God I'll never, *ever*, let you down the way he did. You mean too much to me for that.'

She rocked slightly back and forth, as the sharp wind rushed around her, but she didn't seem to feel the cold now.

She turned away from him, though, still afraid to overcome that one final barrier, still searching for the confidence she needed to throw caution, quite literally, to the wind.

'Oh,' he said behind her, 'you're probably still not convinced that I mean what I say. Well, that's fair enough. I can't offer you any guarantees. But ask yourself something, Nicci; would I have risked my life driving up here from Anderberg if I *didn't* mean what I just said?'

She turned back to him, a battle of wills taking place inside her.

'I *need* you, Nicci,' he said urgently. 'You see all this snow? It practically guarantees a future for the Rose! But unless you're there to share it with me, I might just as well close up shop and go to work for somebody else.'

The train conductor, who had been standing nearby, stepped forward. 'Young man,' he said, addressing Andrew. 'Forgiff me for asking, but . . . are you by any chance proposing to this young lady?'

Andrew glanced at him, thought about it for a moment, then said, 'Yes.' He looked at Nicci once more, and said in a stronger tone, 'Yes. If she'll have me.'

Nicci looked up at him. Of course she wanted him! But dare she take the chance? Could she really tar *every* man with the same brush, as Karen had said earlier?

She knew she could not.

'Andrew,' she said, setting down her luggage. 'I . . . I love you, too.'

She stepped into his waiting arms and he held her close, pressing his lips against the top of her head and whispering promises of love and fidelity that she knew instinctively that he would never break.

Clearing his throat, the conductor

said in a very brisk voice, 'Now, iff you don't mind, we are already running behind schedule.'

Andrew and Nicci glanced up at him just as he blew his nose and blinked tears from his eyes.

'I'm sorry we held you up.'

The conductor gave them a sentimental smile. 'I think we can forgiff you, in the circumstances.'

Within minutes the train was gliding away from the snow-bound station, with Nicci, safe in the arms of the man she loved, watching it leave.

When it was finally out of sight, Andrew bent his head and kissed her tenderly on the lips, and their embrace felt good and right and absolutely wonderful.

'Come on,' he said. 'We've a long drive ahead of us, and an awful lot to sort out.'

'Plans for the Rose?' she asked teasingly.

'Plans for our *wedding*,' he corrected, holding her close.

And arm in arm they trudged back along the platform to the waiting car, their footsteps forming loving, united patterns in the snow.

THE END

Other titles in the
Linford Romance Library:

FOREVER IN MY HEART

Joyce Johnson

With the support of a loving family, Julie Haywood is coping well with the trauma of divorce and the difficulties of single parenthood. Well on track with her medical career, she is looking forward to an exciting new promotion — not realising it will bring her into contact with Rob, a part of her past she has tried to forget. Then, when ex-husband Geoff turns up, Julie finds she has some hard decisions to make . . .

THE SKELTON GIRL

Gillian Kaye

1812: These are tempestuous times in the wool mills of the Pennine moors. Randolf Staines is introducing new machinery to Keld Mill, which will put many of the villagers out of work. Diana Skelton, whose father used to own Keld Mill, takes a strong dislike to Randolf, and when there is trouble amongst the dismissed croppers she becomes involved. It is only after a night of violence at the mill that Diana and Randolf begin to see eye to eye . . .

A NEW LIFE FOR ROSEMARY

Anne Holman

Alone since the loss of her family in an air-raid, Rosemary — newly demobbed from the WRNS — returns to her old home. But she is shocked to find that a whole family has been temporarily housed there . . . With little knowledge of children and cooking, and with housework to do, she has her hands full — especially when strange things begin happening at the bottom of her garden . . . Friends help her cope, as she helps them. But will she also cope when romance calls?